Country Girls 3:

Carl Weber Presents

NOV 16

CH

Country Girls 3:

Carl Weber Presents

Blake Karrington

www.urbanbooks.net

Urban Books, LLC
97 N18th Street
Wyandanch, NY 11798

Country Girls 3: Carl Weber Presents
Copyright © 2016 Blake Karrington

ISBN 13: 978-1-62286-796-7
ISBN 10: 1-62286-796-3

First Trade Paperback Printing November 2016
Printed in the United States of America

10 9 8 7 6 5 4 3 2 1

This is a work of fiction. Any references or similarities to actual events, real people, living or dead, or to real locales are intended to give the novel a sense of reality. Any similarity in other names, characters, places, and incidents is entirely coincidental.

Distributed by Kensington Publishing Corp.
Submit orders to:
Customer Service
400 Hahn Road
Westminster, MD 21157-4627
Phone: 1-800-733-3000
Fax: 1-800-659-2436

Country Girls 3:

Carl Weber Presents

by

Blake Karrington

Chapter 1

Niya inhaled the scent of the train station as the conductor helped her down the steps. It was good to be back in the Queen City. She slung the bag on her shoulder, and began walking up the steps of the train station. As she ascended the stairs she took a deep breath. The air was clean. No scent of urine and shit like Philly. One thing about the South: they will lock your ass up and fine you if you litter. She appreciated the freshness of the South more after being in Philly for a minute. She checked her watch and scanned the street for Diamond.

"Whoever he is he should be ashamed of himself," a man said, smiling at Niya.

"I'm sorry, are you speaking to me?" Niya asked as she checked her phone.

"Yeah. A lady as fine as yourself should, one, not be taking a train and, two, not be waiting for anyone out here on the street."

Niya laughed. It wasn't the worst line she had ever heard. She looked up from her phone and stared into the brown eyes of the tall stranger. As she began to speak, Diamond drove up, blowing the horn.

"Hey, girl! Sorry I'm late but traffic was ridiculous!" Diamond ran to Niya. She wrapped her arms around her, laughing and partly crying. "Dang, you lost weight! Give me your bag, bitch!" Diamond giggled as she threw Niya's bag in the back of the Range Rover.

Niya smiled at the stranger. Although she loved Eagle, it was nice to be noticed by a fine-ass dude with a little swag. He walked over and opened the door for her. She stepped inside and, without another word, he closed the door. He adjusted his white baseball cap and walked toward the parking lot. Niya watched him in the rearview mirror until he disappeared among the cars.

"Really? Damn, I think I got some napkins in here for you to wipe the drool off your chin!" Diamond said, pretending to look for napkins.

"Girl, shut up. It was nice to be noticed is all."

Diamond chuckled and shook her head. She pulled out to the street. She handed Niya a folder as she merged onto the ramp for I-77.

"What we gonna do?" Diamond asked, looking straight ahead. "Alexus didn't deserve that shit."

"It ain't really about what you deserve. It's about what's dealt to you. It's this fucking life, D. This life ain't meant for you ride off into the sunset or be rocking on your front porch. I'm tired, man. Tired of burying girls, tired of fucking dodging these pigs. I'm just ready to get the hell out of this shit."

Diamond listened to Niya. She had been thinking the same thing. It was time for them to move the hell on while they had a chance to get out. However, this life was not one that just released you, and they had worked too damn hard in building MHB. She was tired of the life, but not tired of her lifestyle. She shook her head as she imagined herself in some type of corporate job. That was not something that was going to happen.

"I feel ya, Niya, but what the hell we gon' do? Just let the fools who killed Alexus think they got away with it? Hell, if we do that they gonna definitely gun for us."

Niya sighed and closed her eyes. Diamond's actions were always tied to her emotions, which usually meant hell for whoever crossed her.

"D, please, let's just focus on the arrangements for Lex. I just want to lay her to rest, see my kids, and then I can move on from there, a'ight?"

"A'ight," Diamond mumbled. "Ni, it's good to have you home, boo."

Niya looked at the Charlotte skyline and exhaled. "Yeah, D. It's good to be home."

Standing on the balcony, Gwen sipped her mimosa and checked her phone. *Diamond and Niya should be arriving soon.* She knew that Niya would be anxious to see the twins, but she had decided against bringing them into the city. MHB had some business to tie up.

"Ay, yo, Gwen!" Porter yelled as he entered the room.

"I'm out here!"

"Hey, I came as soon as I got your message. What's up?" Porter asked as he hugged Gwen. He and Gwen had been friends for over twenty years. He was a straight dude who always made sure that Gwen understood how to play the game, and recently he had been guiding her on how to slowly get out of the game and go legit. Shit, white folks did it all the time. It's how most of the wealthy muthafuckers left inheritance to their children. The government always took niggas' shit, but somehow these white muthafuckers like the Rockefellers and Trumps set their family up for success off the noses and asses of folks.

"So it sounds like you need some big toys," Porter said as he sat down on the lounger beside Gwen.

Gwen continued to stare at the sky, sipping her drink.

"Yeah, well, I told you, getting out sometimes is hard, G. It ain't like you just turn in your resignation letter and they throw you a party. As long as you straddle the line, you gonna have to make sure that you have no issues with being two people. How much you need?"

"I need enough to drag niggas so far to hell that when they think of MHB, they would rather go hide behind Satan than face us," Gwen said with a trembling voice.

Diamond pulled into the parking garage. MHB owned the building, but it was listed under a dummy corporation. They had used a college kid named Brandi to establish a real estate company. Brandi was a naïve kid who was excited to have someone back her business plan for being an interior designer and real estate investor. So she was the perfect cover for them in this location. She was told that this building would be used for corporate banking clients, and that the third parking level would have to have high security clearance.

Diamond surveyed the parking garage. The only car that should be there was Gwen's old Honda that she drove to stay low-key. She spotted the Honda. She tucked the .45 in her waistband. Niya stepped out of the Range with her hand inside her bag, gripping her gun. Diamond had parked near the elevator, so it only took a few minutes for them to get to it and step inside. Niya could feel the anxiety vibrating from Diamond as the elevator began to go up the floors.

"D, I'm gonna need your ass to calm down. Shit, this place is secure, right?" Niya said, watching the numbers light up on the elevator panel.

"Yeah, it's supposed to be, but I ain't trusting shit right now. Better safe than sorry, right?"

The elevator dinged as the doors to the twelfth floor opened. Diamond checked the halls then stepped out. Niya followed her. Niya knew shit was crazy, but to see Diamond on edge like this put her nerves on high alert. They approached the door of the penthouse. Diamond keyed the access code into the pad, and opened the door.

"Gwen!" Diamond yelled. "Look what I got with me!"

Gwen stared at Niya. The two women's eyes locked as they both stood in silence.

"So you just gonna stand there and look at me?" Niya finally said as she walked toward Gwen. As soon as the women hugged, tears began flowing down their cheeks. Diamond joined them, crying and wailing in pain at the loss of their friends and the pressure of being in the game.

"I missed you, Ni," Gwen said as she wiped her eyes. "Sorry you had to come back to this bullshit."

"Seems like some shit is just dropping on me everywhere I turn. Right before I left, I found out that Eagle's aunt was murdered by a damn African. That lady had nothing to do with the game and she got caught in the middle of my shit." Niya walked into the kitchen and poured herself a glass of orange juice. "So Nose did this shit to Lexus?"

"Muthafucka had the audacity to be in my house right before he murked her. So when do we move on these niggas?" Diamond said as she poured herself a glass of Goose.

"Little early for that?" Gwen said, shaking her head.

Niya noticed something move on the balcony. She looked questioningly at Gwen.

"Chill. That is Porter. He getting the heat that we gonna need to handle this business. Nose thinks he running shit, and I'm sho' he got niggas ready to blast us out for revenge. We need all the allies we can get right now."

"I'm not sure I'm up for this shit, G. I think we all just need to head out, man. It is time for us to step back. This shit is too much. Hell, Eagle's aunt got caught up in our shit in Philly."

"Damn, who did it?"

"Fucking Africans. But I will worry about that later. Let's handle this shit first. Let's lay our girl to rest."

Chapter 2

The heavy aroma of burning marijuana drifted through the air and into Mac's nose, immediately waking him from his sleep. He cracked his eyes open and looked for Spring, who was supposed to be asleep beside him; but she wasn't in the bed. As soon as he lifted his head off the pillow to further investigate the familiar smell, the sound of a gun being cocked back made his heart jump. He slowly turned over onto his back and moved his eyes to the source of the sound.

Sitting in a chair across the room was a slim man wearing a black hoodie with a semiautomatic pistol in his right hand. The man was clean cut, but he had a look in his eyes that said he wasn't afraid to pull the trigger.

"Damn, homie, what's all this about?" Mac sat up and rested his back against the headboard of the bed.

The man didn't say anything. Instead, he just leaned back in the chair and placed the gun on his lap. Mac could hear Spring coming up the stairs. It sounded like she was talking on the phone to somebody.

He seized this opportunity to warn her. "Spring, get out of the house. It's somebody in here with a gun!" He hoped to alert her and maybe frighten the gunman long enough for him to grab his pistol from the nightstand drawer.

Spring calmly walked into the room while continuing her conversation on the phone. Mac started to caution her again about the man sitting in the corner, but she just waved him off.

"Boy, stop all that damn yelling. You see I'm on the phone," Spring told him right before she ended her call.

The gunman got up, walked up to Spring, and wrapped his arm around her shoulder. Placing a soft kiss on her cheek, he looked over at Mac with a smirk on his face.

"Trey, you're so crazy," Spring said and took the gun from him.

Spring pointed Trey's gun at their latest victim. At that moment, Mac realized that he'd been set up.

"Open the safe, nigga, or you can die wit' ya money. It really don't matter to me," she instructed while waving the pistol at him.

Mac sat there in disbelief, wondering how in the world he had let Spring get so close to him. He never saw it coming. They'd been seeing each other for the past two months and, at this point, he actually considered her to be at the very least wife material.

"Damn, shawty, you was good." Mac smiled and shook his head as he got out of the bed slowly.

Spring kept a close eye on him as he pushed the king-sized bed over to access the floor safe. In the two months Spring was with him, she'd learned just about everything there was to know about Mac, all the way down to the intricate details of his lucrative real estate scam. He carried a lot of cash in his line of work; and, though he didn't keep all of it in one place, Spring knew that the bulk of it was right there.

"Damn, it's crazy 'cause I actually was falling for you," Mac continued while punching the code into the keypad.

His heart raced once he opened the safe and laid eyes on the chrome ten-shot .40-cal resting on top of the money. As Trey made his way over to him, Mac reached in and grabbed the gun. Trey saw what he was doing and tried his best to rush him, but Mac let the bullets fly. He hit Trey with all four shots.

Trey fell onto Mac, and for a few seconds a short struggle ensued until Trey became too weak to fight him and fell unconscious from his wounds. When Mac pushed his body to the side, he looked up just in time to see Spring aiming her gun at him. Not giving him a chance to make another move, she pulled the trigger, pumping a single bullet into his chest. Mac's body fell backward and blood spewed out of his mouth and onto the floor. His body started to convulse, and instantly he went into cardiac arrest.

Spring jumped down and attempted to give Trey CPR, but she soon realized that it was too late.

"No," she whispered.

The pain in her chest was unbearable. Seeing that there was nothing else she could do for Trey, she closed his eyelids before she stood up. Stepping over Mac's convulsing body, she went straight to the safe. She began to remove the stacks of money, periodically looking over at Trey's lifeless body. Choking back the tears, knowing he'd want her to finish the job, she cleaned out the safe in a couple of minutes. She also got the small glass display case where Mac kept all of his jewelry.

Spring hated the fact that she had to leave Trey behind, but she knew she had no other choice. He was dead and there wasn't anything she could do about it. She bagged up the cash and the jewelry then left the house. Finally letting the tears drop, she inhaled deeply at the thought of just losing her mentor and friend.

Summer typed away on her laptop as the professor gave his lecture on psychology and all of the key points students needed to know for an upcoming exam. Her childhood dream of becoming a psychiatrist was starting to feel within reach, as this was her last year in college.

The work was hard and the study hours were long. Sleep was hard to come by as well, especially trying to maintain a job amid it all.

"That will end today's class. I will see you guys on Monday," Professor Hicks concluded.

Students rushed out of the lecture hall in packs and, after typing up the rest of her notes, Summer packed up her things and got out of dodge. As soon as she stepped outside, she knew exactly how she was going to spend her weekend.

"Summer," an all-too-familiar voice yelled out from the crowd.

When Summer turned her head, she saw her mother, Ms. Gloria, pushing her way through the students until she reached her baby.

"Mom, what are you doing here?" Summer asked, giving her mother a hug and a kiss.

"Well, you can at least act like you're happy to see me," Ms. Gloria joked. "I'm here because I wanted you to come home for the weekend. I'm having Sunday dinner and I want you and ya crazy sister to be there."

Summer was originally from Philly, but she attended the University of North Carolina at Chapel Hill when her mom and sister migrated to Charlotte a couple of years ago. It was a shock to see her mother travel that far.

Growing up in Philly, Sunday dinner was a very important part of black culture. Summer had been so busy in school that she'd missed out on at least six months' worth of dinners. Ms. Gloria had her mind set and she refused to go another Sunday without Summer there. With that explanation, along with a little guilt trip, Summer decided that she could manage Sunday dinner with the family.

"So, you haven't met any nice boys out here?" Ms. Gloria asked as they made their way to the campus parking lot.

Summer knew the question was coming. She smiled and shook her head. "There are a few nice guys out here, but I ain't got time to be seeing anybody right now."

She was definitely telling the truth. Her schedule was way too hectic to even consider dating anyone. All Summer had time for was a boy toy, one she wasn't about to tell her mother about. Trying to avoid an interrogation, she quickly changed the topic.

"So, how is she?" Summer asked about her twin sister, whom she hadn't seen in months.

"Oh, well, you know Spring. Out living the glamorous street life." Ms. Gloria sighed before unlocking her car door. "I worry about that girl. She's out there ripping and running around in the streets doing God knows what. The bank called me the other day and told me that the house was paid off in full and the deed was in the mail. That crazy girl done came up with forty-five thousand dollars and paid off the remaining balance."

"Well, isn't that a good thing?" Summer asked.

"It would be if I knew where she got that money from. She ain't got no job, and she damn sure didn't hit the lottery. And I swear if I find out she's selling drugs, I'm calling the cops on her my damn self!" Ms. Gloria threatened.

Summer looked over at her mom and couldn't help but laugh at how serious she tried to be. She knew that no matter what Spring did, her mother wouldn't go that far. The love she had for her twin girls was too strong. After a few seconds, Ms. Gloria had to laugh at her own words.

"I'll talk to Spring when I see her," Summer assured Ms. Gloria before they finally pulled into traffic.

Summer's phone trilled. The number was one she didn't recognize, and the area code was 980. She paused a moment as her finger hovered over the ignore button. She swiped left.

"Hello? Yes, this is Summer Ortiz. Alexus? What? Are you sure?" Summer's stomach tightened, as bile rose in her throat.

Gloria looked over at her. She noticed the color drain from her face. "What? What's wrong? Is it your sister?"

Summer was unable to answer her mother's questions. She had a large lump in her throat, and she felt she would vomit at any moment.

"Summer!" Gloria yelled as she crossed three lanes of traffic to get to the emergency lane. Gloria swerved across the far right lane, barely missing an SUV. She hit the brakes as soon as she entered the emergency lane.

"Summer," Gloria said, trying to speak in a calmer voice.

"No. Spring is okay as far as I know. That was a call from a Detective Carter. She said that Alexus has been murdered. She found my number on her emergency contact list in her phone."

Gloria felt the air leave the car. Alexus was the only thing she had left of her brother. She was a sweet girl, always helpful, and respectful. They would see her from time to time around holidays. She knew she had recently gotten into real estate, and was doing quite well for herself. "What happened?"

"I don't know all the details, but me and Spring will find out, Mama. God, I can't believe she is gone."

"You said that she said that she was murdered?" Gloria asked as she put the car in drive.

"That is what she said. It was a homicide," Summer said as she looked in the glove compartment for a tissue. "God, probably some asshole she showed a house to or something."

Gloria merged back onto the interstate. They both rode in silence as they headed down the interstate. Summer's heart ached. She put on her sunglasses, hiding the tears that flowed from her eyes.

"When we get to the house, me and Spring will go down to the station to find out what happened."

Chapter 3

"You good, babe?" Niya asked Eagle. She was worried about him, not because of the danger from the Africans but more with regard to their relationship. If she would not have been so greedy, she may have prevented the Africans from looking for blood. Killing that African bastard didn't seem to be the wrong move at the time, but now she was really regretting her choice. Eagle sounded distant and cold as he spoke to her. "I love you, Eagle. Be safe."

"I always am," Eagle said before hanging up.

"Ma'am, if you are ready we can go over the arrangements now," the stout white man said sympathetically, smiling at Niya, Gwen, and Diamond.

"Yeah, sorry. We are ready," Niya said as she followed the man into the large white office. They took a seat in the large plush white chairs that were placed in front of the large desk.

"So everything you asked for has been arranged. The only thing we need now is the body, which I am told isn't being released due to the ongoing investigation. "

"Yes, Mr. Hover, I am aware of that," Gwen said as she slid dark shades off her face and crossed her legs. She stared directly into his eyes. "It is my understanding you work very closely with the homicide unit in the county. I'm sure a man of your stature has developed quite a reputation with them." Gwen uncrossed her legs and made sure to let her pencil skirt slide farther up her thighs in the process. The movement quickly caught Mr. Hover's attention.

"Yes, we were hoping you might be willing to call in a few favors and have the body released to you by tomorrow morning," Niya said as she pouted her lips and gave him her most innocent face.

"Mr. Hover, we were practically sisters, and it would mean a lot to us if you could get her body released," Diamond chimed in. She had made her way next to Mr. Hover and was leaning in toward him, rubbing her breast along his arm as she spoke. Mr. Hover had gotten so distracted with Niya and Gwen that the sudden feeling of Diamond brushing up against him completely caught him off guard. Gwen pulled out a large brown envelope and slid it across his desk.

Mr. Hover opened the envelope to discover stacks of hundred-dollar bills neatly tied up.

"Girls, I will do my best to have the body released by tomorrow morning," he said as he placed the envelope in his top drawer.

"Thank you, Mr. Hover; and please remember to make this as discreet as possible. We will be sending some security with you when you retrieve the body. As we stated earlier, we are not sure who did this or why. We want to take every precaution to protect the family and your workers from any harm," Gwen stated.

Mr. Hover simply nodded in agreement. Gwen put on her Grace Kelly shades. She shook Hover's hand and the women left the funeral home.

Diamond opened the passenger door of the Hummer. Tito sat with his usual scowl on his face. He started the Hummer. Gwen and Niya got into the back seat. Tito checked the rearview mirror, waiting for Niya to approve him pulling away.

"Señorita Niya?"

"Oh, yeah, Tito, we ready to go," Niya said as she stared at the lake.

"Not good news from Philly?" Gwen asked as she opened a bottle of water.

"I don't know. I did some shit before I left that caused some problems. Niggas in Philly is a little different from QC folks. Philly locked by African families, and they everywhere. I pissed off one of their little fuck niggas."

"Pissed them off how?"

"Smoked one of their damn brothers just making my moves. Now dude out for blood. He killed Eagle's aunt with a fucking hammer. That old lady ain't ever hurt nobody, and she was all that Eagle had left."

"We really want to go to war on this shit, Niya? I say we just get the hell out of here."

"We can't leave this shit right now, Gwen," Diamond spit. "Those niggas got to pay for what they did to Alexus. They need to pay for the disrespect they showed by coming in my fucking house. We MHB, and they need to learn what that means. We ain't going nowhere until these muthfuckas are breathing dirt."

Detective Jaza Carter stared at the photo of the young woman on the floor. The killer took his time unloading his gun into her body. *MHB. Money Hungry Bitches.* Jaza scoffed. These chicks were the worst group of violent bitches she had ever seen. Miami female kingpins were like kittens compared to what she had seen the women do to protect their drug empire. She had told the coroner to let her know if they came in to claim the body. They had refused to speak to the police, and had ignored all phone calls that she had made to them. Taking down a group like this was a career builder.

"Hey, Carter, what you working?" Thompson said as he sat down at the desk across from her. Beads of sweat were on his forehead. He opened a bottle of water and guzzled it down. The little white fan on his desk hummed as he turned it to high; and he placed his face in the breeze. "It is just too damn hot to be dredging through the fucking projects looking for a damn weapon. Shit, these fools never stop. Damn, take a summer break!"

"Now, Thompson, if they did that what would we have to do?" Carter chuckled.

"Shit, sit by the fucking pool. I haven't even put my toe in my new pool yet. My kids FaceTime me jumping into the pool, so I guess that is something."

"Yeah, well, it is more for them anyway, right?"

Thompson looked at the folder with the letters MHB on the front. "Money Hungry Bitches, huh? Whew, every damn cop in this precinct wants a piece of them. Shit, I was there when they arrested that Niya chick. Tough one, pretty girl, too, but I can tell you that she is a viper! The feds say that they are one of the most violent groups they have every encountered. Taking that crew down is damn near impossible. Damn near killed Borora. He became obsessed with them."

"Yeah, I heard about Borora. Where is he now?" Carter asked as she continued to skim Alexus's file.

"Transferred to Jersey, I think. Shit, I don't know really. A piece of advice to ya: leave that shit to the feds."

"Can't. A body just dropped. Gotta work it."

Thompson opened another bottle of water. He took a big swig from it, and then sat back. "A body?"

"Yeah. An Alexus Jackson. They found her in a trailer shot multiple times. Looks like someone took their time doing it, too."

"She a member or victim?" Thompson said, wiping his forehead.

"Looks like she is a member, although from appearances she was working as a Realtor. There were closing documents on her desk."

"Like mortgages? Well, maybe she wasn't in the game no more?"

"Yeah, and I'm a size two," Carter said sarcastically. "No, whoever did this was angry, and her crew waited to even call it in. Now I can't reach any of them. I was, however, able to find some family. Hopefully they will be able to talk to me."

"Yeah. Don't hold your breath. You know how this plays out. MHB ain't no little street gang. They are organized, smart, and they know how to stay ahead of us. They are also willing to take out anyone who gets in their way, believe me."

Carter stared at the mug shot of Niya. The girl had no soul behind her eyes. She knew she had been released and was MIA at the moment. She didn't have access to a lot of the file due to her security clearance being too low. All she needed to do was talk to Martin in IT, and she would have everything she needed. He owed her favor anyway from making that assault charge he had against him go away. MHB was going to be her ticket to getting to Quantico.

There was silence around the table as Spring, Corey, and Vick mourned the loss of Trey. He wasn't just a part of the Take Down crew; he was also the driving force that made the wheels go 'round. A mastermind in his own right, he'd taught each of them everything they knew about the streets. However, Spring was his protégé. Their relationship was almost familial, and Spring admired him for his wealth of street knowledge and fearlessness. She was now Trey's successor. Spring knew she had to be the leader and call all of the shots.

"Take this to Lou," Spring instructed, speaking of Trey's only child. She pushed the large book bag full of money she had gotten from Trey's house across the table toward Corey. Lou was eighteen years old and fresh out of high school. Spring knew Lou personally and had a lot of love for him, but she couldn't stand to face him at that moment, let alone answer any questions she knew he would have.

"I know this might be a fucked-up time to say this," Vick said, "but we gotta move on that other project before the window of opportunity closes on us."

Spring cut her eyes over at him. Although she was mad and hurt, she knew Vick was telling the truth. Trey was gone and he wasn't coming back; the show had to go on. She didn't want to waste all of the hard work Trey had done on the next sting. If executed correctly, that lick could prove to be in the millions. She refused to let that pass her by.

"I hear you, V, and as much as I want to cuss your ass out right now, you are right. I'll meet up with Gary later on today. But I need you to go over that homework Trey gave you," Spring said.

"And what about the down payment?" Vick pointed to the stacks of money Corey was stuffing into the bag. The money that she'd stolen from Mac was supposed to be the down payment on the sting, but it was just a little short.

"Don't worry about the money. I'll take care of that, too," she replied as her phone vibrated in her pocket.

She pulled it out and saw that a text message had just come through. It was her twin sister, Summer, letting her know that she was on her way to their mother's house. Spring became even more frustrated at the thought of her sister being in the city.

"I have some family stuff I need to deal with right now. But make sure y'all meet me back here around midnight so I can let y'all know what's up."

Corey and Vick nodded as they got up from the table. With everybody having something to do, they all dispersed, but not before grabbing their guns off of the table. In their line of work, being strapped was every bit of mandatory. It was a rule Trey had established for them years ago.

Spring crept through the front door of her mother's house, trying not to be heard. Once she was inside, she gently closed the door behind her and locked it. She couldn't see her, but she knew her mother was somewhere posted in the kitchen because she heard the oldies jams blasting. Spring quietly placed her bag on the floor by the staircase and pulled the Glock 9 mm out of the side pocket before proceeding up the stairs.

She could hear the shower water running in the hallway bathroom and Summer singing along with the music that her mother played downstairs. Walking through the dimly lit hallway, Spring made her way to the slightly ajar bathroom door. Spring entered and walked slowly toward the shower with her gun aimed. When Spring yanked the shower curtain to the side, Summer was standing there, still singing, with a pistol pointing directly back at her. The two women stood there for a second staring into each other's eyes until Summer finally stopped singing.

Spring spoke first. "I thought I told you to call me ahead of time if you planned on coming to the city."

"Well, your mother wanted me to come to Sunday dinner," Summer shot and lowered her gun.

Spring lowered her gun as well and smiled. She couldn't help the fact that she was happy to see her sister. It also pleased her that her sister hadn't forgotten the street instinct that their father had instilled in both of them.

"I thought college life would have made you soft," Spring said to her own lovely mirror.

"Never." Summer smirked. "I don't know who you thought you were, sneaking in here like I'm scared to bust back or something."

After turning off the water and stepping out of the tub, Summer grabbed her towel and wrapped it around herself. She gave Spring a tight bear hug and Spring embraced her back. The only reason Spring was so concerned about Summer being in the city was that she had put in so much work and done so much dirt, she didn't want anybody to mistake Summer for her. Being in the line of work that she was in meant there was always a target on her back. If something happened to Summer because of her own personal mess, she didn't know what she would do.

"Come on, let's go talk to Mama," Spring said. She tucked her gun in the front of her jeans, making sure to drape her loose shirt over it so her mom wouldn't see it, and walked out of the bathroom. On her way out, she nodded to Summer's gun still sitting on the edge of the tub. "Grab that. You know how she feels about guns."

Summer did what her sister said, knowing that she was right, and hurried to dry her body off. She put lotion on, then threw on the shorts and T-shirt she'd brought in the bathroom with her. After she was done, she let her sister lead the way. The girls were identical. The only thing that distinguished them from each other was a tiny birthmark on the top of Spring's foot. Other than that, no one would ever be able to tell them apart. Half black and half Puerto Rican, the twins' skin complexion was golden brown, smooth, and very soft to the touch. They both had long, straight jet-black hair and stood five feet five inches equally, and weighed 140 pounds. Spring's ass was slightly rounder, and Summer's breasts were a little larger, but it was nothing that the average eye could catch.

"Hey, before we go downstairs, I got some bad news today," Summer said, leaning on the rail.

"What?" Spring said as she checked herself out in the full-length mirror on the wall.

"Alexus is dead," Summer said.

Spring's legs became weak as she slid down the wall onto the top step. "Dead? What? How?"

"I don't know. A homicide det—"

"Homicide? What, you mean she was murdered?"

Summer nodded. She could see the wheels turning in Spring's head. She could also feel the anger rising in her. Being mirror twins they often shared emotional experiences. Earlier today Summer felt a strong pain in her chest. It was brief, but long enough to make her a little alarmed.

"They want me to come down to the station, since I am listed as an emergency contact in her phone and on some form she had at the hospital."

"Shit, we gotta go to the police station? You know that's gonna be a little hard for us to do."

"Well, I'm not going alone. I'm staying with Mom, remember? I will go down there with her."

"Yeah, like that is going to work," Spring scoffed. Today was really a fucked-up day for her. She had lost her mentor and a cousin in the same day. "I mean, we have the same face, stupid."

"Yeah, but not the same ID, and as far as they know I've been in college, and they have no idea where you are. Besides, I don't think you will be a focus right now. We gotta go get our family," Summer said as she began to walk down the stairs. "Come on, let's try to cheer Mommy up."

They came down the stairs as quietly as they could. Tiptoeing into the living room, they tried to surprise their mother.

"What in the world!" Ms. Gloria exclaimed, stopping at the kitchen door. She looked into the living room and was shocked to see Spring standing next to Summer.

"Who am I?" Spring asked with a smile on her face.

For kicks, Summer also smiled. When they were younger, they used to always play the "Guess Who" game with their parents. Their dad could never tell them apart, but Ms. Gloria had never gotten it wrong.

"Dumb and Dumber." Ms. Gloria laughed. She walked up and placed her hand on the side of Spring's face. "Where did you get that money to pay off my house?" she asked Spring.

Summer opened her eyes wide and snuck off into the kitchen to check on the food.

"Mom, you worry too much. You don't have to worry about paying ya mortgage anymore, so relax. Okay?"

Ms. Gloria took in a deep breath then shook her head. She loved her girls and didn't want anything to happen to either of them. "I'm just worried about you, baby. This world is a cruel place, and I don't want you getting sucked up into it!"

"Mama, you don't have to worry. I'm gonna be all right," Spring assured her. "Just trust me."

Ms. Gloria smiled then kissed Spring on her forehead. She looked into Spring's eyes. "I trust you, baby; it's the other fool I worry about."

Gloria hugged her daughter tightly. Her heart was aching thinking about Alexus. She was glad her brother wasn't here to see this happen to his baby. Alexus was like her third daughter up until she lost her father. As the years passed she gradually drifted away, occasionally visiting on a holiday here and there. She shared very little about her life, but between her and Spring, the two of them always managed to drop off large sums of money. Now with Alexus being dead, it made her concerned about how Spring had acquired the money for her house. She wanted to press the issue more, but she didn't. She also couldn't deny the fact that she was relieved to finally fully own her home. No more giving up half her check to cover the payments; nor did she have to go through with the plan of doing a reverse mortgage to pay for Summer's college tuition. She showed tough love, but she was grateful to have Spring as her daughter. It touched her heart that her daughter cared that much about her.

"Come on, let's have some girl time. We got a lot to discuss today." Ms. Gloria led Spring into the kitchen so they could eat and talk.

Summer stood in front of the police station staring at the doors. Her heart was racing as she walked up the steps. She paused before stepping on the black mat. A large man walked past her, causing the doors to whoosh open. The cool air caressed her face. She exhaled and walked inside. She had decided to come alone, and allow Spring some time with their mother. She could tell that both of them were too fragile to handle this right now.

"Hi, my name is Summer Ortiz. I am here to see Detective Carter."

"Okay, one second," the female officer said, picking up her phone. After a few brief moments, she told Summer to have a seat. Summer sat in the plastic green chair. She looked up at the skylight. It was late afternoon, but the temperature was still in the high eighties.

"Summer?" Detective Carter asked with her hand extended.

"Yes," Summer answered.

"I am so sorry for your loss. You were listed on an old form of hers at the hospital. We have been trying to contact her business associates, but they haven't returned our phone calls."

"Really? That is odd. Why would they not call you back? Who found her body?"

"One of her business associates reported it to us. We need to follow up with them for some more questions but we have not been able to catch up with them," Detective Carter said as she held the door for Summer. There was a definite odor on this floor. Summer tried to breathe through her mouth. The strong smell of chemicals and human bodies was overwhelming.

"Are you ready for this?" Detective Carter asked before pressing a blue button on the wall.

Summer nodded her head. The large flat screen lit up, and Alexus's face showed on it. Her skin had a gray color to it, and the rest of her body was covered by a white sheet. Summer stared at her cousin. She touched the screen, and bowed her head.

"That is Alexus. God, who would do something like this to her? She wasn't a violent person. She worked in real estate. This is crazy," Summer said, turning away from the screen.

Detective Carter bit her lip, something she usually did when she was anxious. Alexus being a member of MHB meant she had to violent. These women were sociopaths, and even though she didn't have a lot on Alexus, she knew that the woman couldn't have been no damn angel. She wondered if Summer really had no idea about the life Alexus was leading. Summer seemed to be genuinely surprised that her cousin died violently.

"Maybe you can help me get in contact with her business associates," Carter said as she opened the door, and proceeded down the long gray hall.

Summer's ears were ringing as they walked back to the elevator. Seeing her cousin on that slab broke her heart, but it also made her blood boil. Although Alexus appeared to be a good girl, she knew that, like the rest of her family, Alexus stayed strapped. Her mind was also racing with wanting to figure out who would hate her cousin so much that they murdered her in cold blood like that. As far as she knew, Alexus was taking her chance at real estate and trying to make a name for herself in the business world.

"We should be able to release the body to your family by tomorrow," Carter said as she handed Summer a tissue.

"Thank you," Summer said as she wiped her eyes.

"I do have a few questions for you. I know this is a hard time for you, but we need all the help we can get right now to find whoever is responsible for this," Carter said as she pulled a large wooden chair out for Summer. Summer's phone trilled. Spring's picture flashed on the screen.

"Please excuse me one moment. This is my mother."

Carter smiled as Summer swiped her screen and walked back into the hall.

"You a'ight?" Spring asked.

"Yeah, I'm good. I'm gonna talk to the detective to see what I can find out. I'll call you back when I get to the car."

"Hurry up. You making me nervous being down there." The line clicked. Summer walked back into the office.

"Sorry, Detective Carter. This isn't easy for my mother."

"I know this is hard for you and your family. I'm going to do everything I can to find out who did this to your cousin. I have a few questions with regard to her workplace. Does MHB mean anything to you?"

"I think that was the name of the realty company? She seemed to be really happy working there. We had not seen much of her over the last few years. She would always try to stop by on holidays. Can you tell me what happened?"

"Well, one of her associates called it in to us. We got there to find her dead. They seemed to be pretty upset, but we are having a hard time tracking them down for additional questions. Have they been by to see the family?"

"No. You were the first and only person to contact us about Lex. Do you think they had something to do with her murder?" Summer asked.

"No, they are not suspects, but we need to talk to them."

Chapter 4

Niya kissed the twins good-bye. She inhaled their scent, and squeezed them tightly. She buckled them in their seat belts, fighting back her tears of joy and of sadness. They were older, and their questions were more inquisitive. Each time she advised of something that wasn't quite true, they would stare at her with large, curious eyes.

The black SUV made its way out of the parking deck level. She had enjoyed having her babies in her arms, and tucking them in last night.

Gwen and Diamond flashed the lights of the gray SUV before pulling out of the parking deck. Niya threw her bag into the back of the BMW. The 5 Series was not what she was accustomed to driving, which meant it would not draw any attention to her. She would drive down to Tennessee and settle there for a couple of weeks. This would allow the twins time to finish school, and also give her enough time get things in order for their arrival. Leaving the Carolinas behind pained Niya, but it was a necessary step for her and her kids.

Carter munched on a turkey sandwich as she pored over the MHB files while on hold with the receptionist from the coroner's office. So far she had gotten possible names of people in the real estate office and was waiting to hear if anyone besides Summer had shown up to try to identify the body. She'd been working nonstop since the case landed on her desk, and she was determined to find out what happened. If Alexus's murder was tied in to MHB how she thought it was, this case would take her career to the next level.

"What do you mean the body's gone?" Carter yelled at the receptionist when she got the news. She gulped her strawberry soda. "Who released the body?" Carter barked. "I told you nothing was to happen without me approving it first!" Carter snapped as she hung up the phone. She grabbed her gun and rushed out of the office. She wanted to see the video of who picked up the body. She knew that Summer's family couldn't have picked it up so quicky. Summer had just been there less than twenty-four hours ago.

"What the hell, Jackson? I thought I made myself clear that you were to call me before releasing the body! Who signed for it?" Carter snarled as she entered the morgue.

Jackson stepped back as she stormed toward him. "Look, I was on lunch when it was released to Benton Services yesterday. My assistant says that they had the needed paperwork signed by the family."

"What? That is impossible. If it was released yesterday, that means her cousin had just left maybe an hour before the body was released!"

"Look," Jackson said, turning red partly from anger, and partly from embarrassment. "We held that body legally as long as we could. We don't investigate the living down here."

Carter snatched the folder from Jackson. She had to track that body down.

Corey pulled up to Lou's house and let out a sigh when he saw Lou sitting out on the front steps smoking a blunt. At that moment, he could see why Spring didn't want to do what she'd sent him to do. Lou's face held a look of devastation, and Corey knew the loss of his father was what had put it there.

"Wassup, li'l man?" Corey walked up the driveway with the book bag over his shoulder. He didn't know how the conversation would go.

"Damn, Corey, you still call me that?" Lou took in a long, hard pull of the Grand Daddy Kush.

Corey smiled and took a seat right next to him on the steps. He opened his mouth to speak, but before he could get a word out, Lou interrupted him.

"Man, I already know what you're about to say, Corey. You're sorry for my loss, whatever I need you got me, my pops was a good man, and so on. All that shit is cool, but the only things I wanna know are who did it, and where can I find him?" Lou looked over at Corey with a straight face.

"The nigga who did it is already dead," Corey answered.

"Cool. So what about his wife? His kids? Or what about his mom and his pops? Are they still alive? If so, they won't be for long."

Lou was in his feelings. He wanted to kill off Mac's whole bloodline. Corey wasn't surprised one bit. Lou was young and more of the quiet type, but those were the guys who were the most dangerous. Trey was the same way, so he knew what his son was capable of. Corey wasn't going to let Lou go out like that, though.

"There's nobody else to kill," Corey said. He took the book bag off his shoulder and gave it to Lou.

"What is it?" Lou set the bag to the side without even looking in it. "I hope it's that nigga's head."

"Nah. Spring told me to bring that to you. She had to take care of something, but she said that she'll be by as soon as she can." When Lou didn't say anything back, Corey sighed. "Look, Lou, I know you're going through it right now, and I know you might not want to hear this, but I'm here for you. You hear me?" Corey nudged Lou's side to get his attention.

Lou nodded after taking another drag of the blunt; and then he passed it to Corey. For the next hour or so, they sat on the steps blowing blunt after blunt, not saying a word. They both reminisced about Trey and thought about how much he was going to be missed by all.

"'I've done a lot of shit just to live this here lifestyle!'" Young Thug's voice came through the speakers of Spring's gray 2015 Range Rover as she whipped a corner, coming up on her destination. She came to a stop at Max's Carwash on Market Street and placed the car in neutral. Spring allowed the attendant to direct her and she unlocked the car doors. Before her vehicle made it into the washing machine, a hooded man opened the door and hopped into the passenger seat.

"I hope you got my money." He removed the hood from his head. "You was supposed to have it today."

"I know, Gary, but something came up. Trey's dead." Spring turned her head toward him.

"A'ight, so I guess we're done." Gary started to get out of the car, but Spring grabbed his arm before he could.

"Wait! Hold on for a second. Me and my crew, we still wanna do it. I just need another day or two to come up with the money," she explained.

Gary knew that he should snatch his arm away and keep it pushing, but he entertained the conversation. He had always liked Trey, and he knew that Trey had taken a special liking to Spring. Truth be told, he really needed the money, but he was a very calculating person. He liked everything to be on schedule. He wasn't about to do anything until he was paid all of his money up front. It was a fact that Trey had masterminded the plan, but it was Gary who ultimately held the keys to their success. Without him, the sting wasn't going to happen, and Spring was well aware of that.

"No more than two days," she added quickly. Her car was getting to the end of the wash cycle.

Gary sat in silence until they reached the end of it. He threw his hood back over his head and reached for the door handle. "I'll give you until tomorrow night," Gary said and jumped out of the SUV without giving Spring a chance to respond.

There wasn't much that she could've said. He'd said what he said, and the only thing left to do was come up with Gary's money. She didn't know how she was going to come up with $300,000, but she was going to figure it out.

Summer sat in front of her laptop, staring at the screen. The letters MHB scrolled across the top of the screen. Her search had yielded several businesses and articles. MHB Realty was apparently a very successful business. There were numerous articles detailing their quick rise to be one of the top realty companies in the South. They owned everything from business locations, industrial buildings, regular houses, and even land under development contracts. From the looks of things, her cousin Alexus was doing very well for herself working with the company. On the other hand, Summer also learned that MHB stood for Money Hungry Bitches. MHB was a very large group of organized women. She began reading the articles about their organization and how they were suspected of numerous drug operations throughout North and South Carolina, but the authorities had never been able to get enough evidence to bring them down. The only member to have ever been incarcerated was their leader, Niya X, who had been sentenced and released from prison for racketeering charges. There was little to nothing about them mentioned on social media, which meant that they were smart. All information about them was written by the press. She thought back to the diamond necklace that Alexus wore around her neck with the letters MHB. When she and Spring asked her about it, she would just change the subject. After learning about the organization, Summer knew that her cousin had to have been involved with MHB. Summer needed to find these women and find out what they knew about Alexus's murder.

Chapter 5

Summer sat in the passenger seat of Spring's vehicle, smiling from ear to ear. She was always happy to be with her sister, so when Spring asked her to stay with her for the weekend, she jumped at the offer. It would be her first time seeing her sister's new house.

"What are you over there smiling at?" Spring asked.

"I still can't believe that you got a Range Rover and a damn new house. And I'm not even going to ask how you got them."

"Good, 'cause I wasn't going to tell ya ass anyway," Spring said with a smirk. "You know, while you're here, we might as well go see Daddy. It's been a minute, and I know he wants to see us."

Big Rick, the twins' father, was serving a twenty-year sentence in the fed for armed robbery and had been in for about twelve years. The twins were thirteen when he left, but they loved him no less and made it their business to be there for him as much as they could. Big Rick had been a good father when he was home and he spoiled his family to death. The twins would never forget those days. No matter what, he did what he had to do to provide for his family, like any real man would.

"So, what made you move all the way out here?" Summer asked as she watched the scenery change from the city to the suburbs.

"I had to get out of the hood. I can't rest my head where I do all my dirt. Plus, once I had the money to buy my own house, I went for it," Spring explained. "There is nothing in the world like having ya own. It's the best feeling there is."

Summer could definitely agree with that.

"So, here we are," Spring said as she turned down the street she lived on.

There were only ten houses total on the block, five on each side. The houses were huge and beautiful. Each had a two-car garage and long driveways. Spring drove slowly to avoid a couple of kids playing outside in the street. Summer smiled at them as they passed. She was in awe of the neighborhood, and her heart fluttered when they pulled into Spring's driveway. She jumped out the vehicle almost as soon as it stopped, and ran toward the two-story house.

"Hurry up!" Summer yelled at sister. "You're moving too slow! Come unlock the door."

Once Spring caught up to her and unlocked the door, she had to step aside to avoid getting run down by her excited sister. The four-bedroom, three-and-a-half bath home was gorgeous, and Summer couldn't believe that Spring lived there. It was plush. Hardwood floors throughout. Leather sectional couches and recliners in the living room, a large oak wood table in the dining room with matching oak wood china cabinets, and in the kitchen were state-of-the-art stainless steel appliances. The master bedroom was located in the back of the house on the ground level. It had its own bathroom and an access door to a small terrace. A hard cedar wood deck led straight to an in-ground swimming pool.

"Damn, sis, how much did this place cost you?" Summer asked.

"I'm on a twenty-year mortgage and I pay fifteen hundred a month. I plan on paying it off way before then, though."

"I only dream about shit like this. I think I might be pursuing the wrong line of work," Summer said.

Spring walked up beside her, rested her hand on Summer's shoulder, and stared into her sister's eyes. "Nah, sis, stay in college and do ya thing. This life I'm living isn't anything that you want. In an instant, it can all be taken away. I might need to lean on you one day."

Summer could see the sincerity in her sister's eyes. She'd been meaning to ask Spring if she knew about Alexus's involvement with MHB, and now was the perfect time to ask.

"Spring, have you heard of MHB?"

"The realty company Alexus was working for?" Spring broke eye contact.

"C'mon, Spring, don't play dumb with me. I did my research, and I know what MHB is all about. Did you know Alexus was with them?"

"Yes, I did."

"How could you not tell me, Spring? Why do you always keep secrets from me?" It was obvious Summer was hurt.

"Summer, it's not like that. Alexus told me a while back, but we both decided it was best not to tell you." Spring grabbed her twin's hands and looked into her eyes again. "Spring, you're not like me and Alexus. You don't belong in the streets. You were always the one with book smarts, and Alexus and I just weren't made for that."

"Okay, I get that I'm not tough and have that street mentality, but that doesn't mean you guys have to leave me out of things all the time. Alexus is gone now, and I feel like I never knew who she really was," Summer said as she looked down at the floor.

"First of all, don't say that you're not tough. You may not be in the streets like I am, but we have the same blood running through our veins, so I know if push comes to shove, you have what it takes to get shit done."

Spring squeezed Summer's hands. "And second of all, of course you knew her, Summer. She's the same person we grew up with: funny, loving, and a gangster-ass bitch!"

The girls shared a laugh and then Spring became serious again.

"Listen, if that detective calls you asking you any questions about Alexus, you don't tell her anything, okay? When you live by the streets, you gotta let the streets handle your death too. Believe me, MHB's gonna take care of whoever took out our cousin."

"Okay, it's not like I have anything to tell anyway. Mom tried making funeral arrangements to pick up Alexus's body, and she was told at the coroner's office that family on her mother's side had already taken it," Summer said.

Spring immediately knew that was MHB's doing. Alexus didn't have any family outside of them. She decided to leave well enough alone. She had met two of Alexus's friends, Niya and Gwen from MHB, and she was sure the girls would make sure to give Alexus a homegoing she deserved.

"A'ight, good. So look, I gotta go take care of some business in a little bit."

The keys to my Charger are on my nightstand if you wanna go somewhere. Just keep a low profile in the city, and try not to max this out," Spring said and pulled out a Visa.

Summer gave Spring a hug before she walked away. The mall was definitely calling out her name. Summer had to hop in the shower first; then she had a field day in Spring's closet. Being the same size as her sister was always a benefit.

"Carter!" The sound of her superior's voice startled Detective Carter out of her trance. She had been sitting at her desk reviewing the paperwork from Alexus's release. She composed herself and made her way toward Munch's office.

"You called me?"

"Yes, I did," he said without bothering to look up from his desk. "You've been reassigned," he said as he closed the file he'd been reviewing and handed it to Carter.

"What? You're kidding me, right?" she said as she opened the manila folder. "You're putting me on the Robinson case? Munch, this is practically a closed case. This case has been open for almost two years, and all of the traces have gone cold."

"Do you want me to put you behind the desk to help me catch up on some paperwork?"

"No, Munch, but why can't I stay on the case I'm on?" Carter asked, sounding a little desperate.

"That case is no longer within our jurisdiction. Even though the body was found within our parameters, this little lady has been linked to the MHB investigations, and that crosses state borders, making it a federal case." He clapped his hands shut and gave Carter a sarcastic smile.

Carter felt furious and defeated at the same time. She had been working homicides for almost five years, and although she had shown excellent investigative skills and had even solved a few hard cases, she had not been able to garner any recommendations for her to submit an application to work for the FBI. Carter felt like her big break was taken right from under her. She was at a loss for words, and all she wanted to do was get out of Munch's office.

"Can I take the rest of the day off?" she asked.

"You sure can."

With that, Carter grabbed her keys and couldn't get out of the precinct fast enough. She couldn't wait to get her hands on an ice cold beer.

Gary's price of $300,000 up front was high, but as long as Spring got rid of the jewelry she'd taken from Mac, along with the money she had stashed away, she should be able to cover the tab. At times like this, she wished she would have listened to Trey when he told her to stack her money and always keep something nice tucked away for rainy days. Corey and Vick weren't any better with their money. Between the two of them they only had around $80,000 saved up. Combining all of their funds together, they were only short $30,000.

"I'ma go up in here and see what I can get for this shit," Spring told Vick.

She'd picked him up to ride with her to see an old fence she knew at a body shop. It was the perfect cover because nobody would ever think a jewelry fence would be there. The man she was meeting was a Puerto Rican guy named Mike. He was the go-to guy when it came to getting rid of jewelry, and his auto body shop was the place to go.

"Mike, come and get this big-ass dog," Spring yelled from outside.

Mike had a Cane Corso the size of a small horse sitting at the front door of the shop. And for obvious reasons it served its purpose.

"*Cómo estás,*" Mike greeted her, walking out of the garage. He simply commanded the dog to move, then waved Spring over. She was a little hesitant at first, but the dog lay down and didn't seem to care about her presence anymore. Mike led Spring to his office in the back of his shop.

"So, to what do I owe the pleasure?" He took a seat in the chair behind the desk.

"I'm trying to get rid of this," Spring said. She went into her bag and pulled out another smaller bag with the jewelry in it.

Mike dumped the contents out on his desk then began to exam it. It took him every bit of two minutes to come up with a price. "I got ten thousand for everything." Just like a typical fence, he was trying his best to get over.

"Nigga, you crazy," Spring snapped back. "You know I can clear ten racks with just two Rolex watches. I'm trying to get twenty for everything."

Mike immediately declined that offer and gave Spring his final offer. "Look, I got 15K and not a penny more," Mike said. He reached in a drawer and pulled out a stack of money.

Spring knew he meant what he said and she figured that the $15,000 was better than nothing right now. "A'ight, whatever, Mike. You got it."

Mike began to peel off the money and, as he was doing so, a thought came to his head. "I might have another way for you to make some more quick cash," he said.

"Yeah? Well, I'm listening. And don't get any freaky ideas. All the money you've made in ya lifetime couldn't get you this pussy."

Mike chuckled. "I don't pay for pussy, but what you can do for me is simple. I got a small shipment coming in and I need somebody to go and pick it up for me. If you do it, I'll give you another five grand," Mike proposed.

"What is it, and when do you want me to pick it up?"

Mike sat up in his chair. "Let me make a few phone calls. Come back tomorrow morning and I'll have all the info for you." He passed Spring the fifteen grand.

She grabbed the cash, got up, and walked out the front door. No other words needed to be said, and since Spring knew Mike wouldn't have her on a dummy mission, she was down for whatever he needed to be done tomorrow. At the same time, if she could get up another five grand before then, she definitely wasn't going to pass up the offer.

"Damn, you just gon' walk past me like I'm a ghost?" A hand on Summer's arm stopped her in the mall.

She could tell by the way the man was looking at her that he must have mistaken her for Spring. "Boy, shut up," Summer shot back, trying to play it off.

She didn't know if this man was friend or foe, so she pulled out her phone and sent a quick text to her sister: Quick! I'm at the mall, and this guy just approached me. Cute dude, brown eyes, low cut, and two teardrops under his right eye.

Almost as soon as she'd sent the text she got a response back: That's Corey. He's part of my crew, so you're good. Tell him you're there grabbing something and you'll meet him at the spot later.

After Summer sent a quick reply, she put her phone back in her designer bag. It had been awhile since the twins had played games like that on people, but Summer was still on point with it. She turned her attention back to Corey, who was looking at her like she had lost her mind.

"My bad," she said to him. "I was thinking about something somebody sent me on my phone earlier. I didn't even see you."

"You good. So what was Gary talking about?"

"Everything's good. I'm taking care of something right now, but I want you to meet me at the spot later on so we can talk more about everything."

Hearing that, Corey was about to leave, but not before leaning in and giving Summer a kiss on her cheek. It was unexpected, and she almost pulled back. Corey caught the hesitance and raised an eyebrow before he walked off.

Summer looked around the mall to see if anyone had seen the kiss before she strutted off herself. She couldn't do anything but laugh to herself, thinking about how soft his lips were and how good his breath had smelled.

She didn't know if Corey was Spring's boyfriend, but she was definitely going to find out before Corey became any more touchy-feely.

"Damn, girl, you doin' ya thing," Summer said to herself, giving her sister some props on her selection of men.

Big Rick stepped out onto the visiting room floor and his face immediately broke into a grin when he saw Ms. Gloria, Spring, and Summer sitting out there. Seeing the women of his life brought a joyous feeling to him. Any time that he was able to be in the presence of all three of them together was a beautiful thing.

"Hey, baby," Rick said. He gripped Ms. Gloria up first, hugging and kissing her. He loved his twins to death, but his wife always came first when it came to hellos.

"Now which one is you?" He laughed and looked at Spring. He still couldn't tell the girls apart.

"I'm the one who puts five hundred on ya books every month," Spring shot back and leaned in to hug her dad.

"Spring," he replied sarcastically and kissed her on the forehead.

"Hey, Daddy," Summer greeted him, hugging him as well before they all sat down. Summer was like a little kid every time she got around her daddy. And, just like any kid, she asked the only question that was on her mind: "When are you coming home?"

Every time she asked that question, it cut him. "Soon, baby. I'll be home soon. Hopefully before you graduate college," he answered.

"Shit, you need to be worried about this one," Ms. Gloria cut in. "She out here ripping and running the streets like she don't have no sense. You know she paid off our mortgage the other day?"

"Damn, Mom, you telling on me now?" Spring yelled while looking over at Ms. Gloria and rolling her eyes. "You a snitch."

"He's your father and that's my husband, so I can tell him whatever I want about ya narrow behind."

Big Rick looked over at Spring with a stern expression before speaking in an even tone. "Walk me to the vending machine," he instructed before getting up and walking toward the back of the room.

Ms. Gloria stuck her tongue out at Spring and smiled at her when she stood up and followed her dad.

Once Spring and Rick got to the vending machine, his whole attitude changed. He was already well aware of Spring's street life and, though he didn't approve of it, he had to accept it. Spring was stubborn just like him and was going to do whatever she wanted to. Instead of fighting against the current, Big Rick decided that Spring would at least learn the game from him.

"You need to be a little more discreet about ya business out there. There's no way in the world ya mom should be telling me no shit like that, and on top of that, I'm hearing your name mentioned in here," he said. "Clean up your steps a bit. You know better than to move with dirty feet."

Spring hated to be chastised by her father because his opinion of her meant the world. "I'll fix it," Spring said and walked over to the soda machine to get everybody something to drink.

As they were walking back over to Ms. Gloria and Summer, Big Rick put his hand around his daughter's shoulders. "Thank you for handling business, though," Big Rick said, referring to her paying off the house. "Give your mama something less to worry about."

He appreciated and was proud of his daughter for stepping up financially while he'd been locked up. If it weren't for her, things would be harder on everybody. She was the glue holding everything together.

"Yo, my nigga, you think shorty gonna come up with the rest of that bread?" Vick asked as he and Corey sat in Corey's car.

Corey hated when Vick was doubtful and impatient. He could hear it in Vick's voice, and he knew that he was ready to go and take some money right that very second. "Yeah, homie, she gon' come up with it. Just relax."

"Relax? Shit, my money is tied up in this shit. And who the fuck put Spring in charge anyway?" Vick shot back. "I'm a grown-ass man. What the fuck do I look like taking orders from a chick?

Corey gritted his teeth in frustration. "It ain't about taking orders from a chick. Trey could have picked any one of us to be his protégé, but he chose Spring, and he did it for a reason. She's smart."

"So you telling me that this bitch is smarter than you?" Vick attacked. "You think this bitch is smarter than me?"

Corey didn't feel that Spring was smarter than him streetwise, but when it came down to taking money, she had been taught by the best. It was easy to walk up, stick a gun in somebody's face, and demand money, but it took a certain type of person to take the high risks that Trey took. Spring knew Trey before anybody else and had spent the most time with him, so in that area Spring was more of an expert. And because of that, she held an advantage over Corey and Vick. That was the reason Corey didn't take it personally. He knew the game and he knew the rules, and if getting more money meant allowing Spring to take the lead on the scores, then that's what Corey planned to do.

"Yeah, well hopefully this shit pans out," Vick said.

Vick wasn't aware of it, but his loyalty was in question at that point, and Corey was going to keep a sharp eye out on him. Vick was on his last strike, and the next time he jumped out there and did or said something stupid, his spot in their crew wouldn't be guaranteed.

Chapter 6

After Spring wasn't able to come up with the rest of the money on her own, she took Puerto Rican Mike up on his offer. As she had suspected, Mike wanted her to pick up some dope for his brother. The small shipment that he spoke about was actually more than what he'd previously said to Spring, so it was only right that she tack on an extra three grand.

Corey, Spring, and Vick pulled up to the location two cars deep. Vick rode solo while Corey and Spring rode together. Before they went any farther, they all took the time to check the clips of their guns. They had all dabbled in the drug game at different times in life, so they knew what kind of danger came with that world.

"Let's get this shit and get out of there," Spring told Corey as she got out of the car.

The compact black and gray .45 automatic went into her back pocket and then she proceeded to the ware-house door. Vick stayed behind as instructed, standing out in front of the car with an AR-15. The area looked deserted, and though Mike was somewhat trustworthy, Spring wasn't really feeling it.

Spring knocked on the door, and in seconds the large gray door opened up on the side. Two black Cadillac Escalades were parked on the other side, surrounded by several armed men. Once Spring and Corey entered, the doors closed behind them.

"Damn, Mike said you were pretty, but that was an understatement," someone said. The man made his way around the Escalade to get a better look at Spring. "My name is Luv." He stuck his hand out for a shake.

Spring didn't tell him her name. However, she did accept his hand. "I'm trying to get straight to business." She took the duffle bag off Corey's shoulder. "I have money machines in the car if you need to count it."

Luv nodded to one of his boys, who then went to retrieve the goods. It was in a duffle bag much larger than the one the money was in.

"It's all there," Luv told her.

Spring trusted very few people. She unzipped the bag and grabbed one of the plastic-wrapped bricks. After testing its weight in her hand, she jammed a small pocket knife into it. The content on her knife was quickly put into a small glass jar with a solution inside. It tested positive for heroin and, from the coloration of it, the grade was high.

"I'll tell Mike you send your regards," Spring said. She tossed the kilo back into the bag and zipped it up.

Corey tossed the bag over his shoulder and they both turned around and walked out of the warehouse without any further conversation. As they were about to get into the car, one of Luv's boys came out of the warehouse and waved Spring down. She stood between her open driver-side door with one hand behind her back, clutching her gun.

"Luv said to hold on to this." The guy held out a prepaid cell phone.

Spring looked at the device strangely and didn't take it.

"Trust me, you might want to take this," the guy told her.

Only so they could get out of there without any further issues, Spring took the phone and shut the car door.

Puerto Rican Mike lifted his head up when he heard the bell ring at the front desk. He and Santana, one of his boys, were right in the middle of connecting the wires to an engine they had just installed. He knew the deal with Luv wasn't going to take that long, so he figured Spring was back.

"Stay," he told his dog, who was anxious to answer the door for him.

To his surprise, it wasn't Spring at the desk, but a cute chick who was just as sexy as she was.

"How can I help you?" Mike asked. Looking over her shoulder, he saw what appeared to be the woman's car sitting out front with the hood up.

"My car won't start back up," she replied in a soft and innocent voice.

"Let me take a look at it," Mike said.

He came around to the front, and as he was making his way outside, the female walked closely behind him. In the matter of a split second, she drew a .380 automatic from her waist, pointed it at the back of Mike's head, and pulled the trigger.

Mike's body fell face first to the ground. He died instantly. The shot caught the attention of Santana, and he along with the dog jumped into action.

The female stepped over Mike's body and was heading to the car when, out of nowhere, it felt like a car hit her from behind. The Cane Corso knocked her to the ground and began to gnaw on her, starting with her right breast. He ripped it clean off of her chest plate, then he latched on to her arm when she tried to grab her face. He shook the girl like a rag doll. She even managed to get off a shot at him, but the small caliber did little damage. The dog went straight for her face, then her neck, growling as he bit chunks of flesh from her face. Her screams were muffled when he locked on to her neck. He didn't have to be trained to do what he did to the girl. He shook her by the neck and dragged her lifeless body all over the garage.

Santana stood there and did nothing while the huge dog had his way with the girl. Standing over Mike's dead body, he felt like she got the death that she deserved. It was a vicious but swift retaliation. Now the only question left was why all of it had happened.

"What da hell is he doing?" Spring said.

In her rearview mirror, Vick's headlights blinked on and off. It looked like he wanted her to pull over, so as soon as Spring got the chance, she did so right in the middle of Harris Boulevard. Vick jumped out of his car and walked up to Spring's window.

"What's going on?" Spring asked when she rolled her window down. She could tell by the look on his face that he was on one.

"Yo, that's a lot of dope in that bag. I say fuck Mike and break that shit down," Vick said.

"Nah, you trippin'," Spring shot back.

"Come on, Spring, we're takers. That's what we do. Do you know how much money we can get off that shit?"

Spring looked over at Corey. "Can you believe this shit?" she said before she turned back to Vick. "Is that what you wanted me to pull over for?"

For Corey, it didn't matter what they did with the dope. He was riding with whatever Spring decided. He kept his eyes on Vick.

"This conversation is over. I'm not even going to entertain ya thoughts right now," Spring said and rolled up her window.

Vick was furious, especially when she pulled off on him. He ran back to his car, jumped in, and sped off right behind her. When Spring got to the traffic light on Harris and Old Statesville Roads, Vick pulled his car in front of hers, blocking her in. She reached for her gun in the center console and so did Corey. Vick surprised both of them when he jumped out of his car with the AR-15 in his hand.

"Don't play yourself," Vick yelled as he walked around to Spring's car.

"Fuck that nigga," Corey said as he reached for the door handle.

Spring grabbed his arm and nodded at the cop car that was coming through the intersection. The officer had to do a double take, thinking that his eyes were playing tricks on him. Spring looked Vick in his eye and then pointed at the cop car that approached him from behind. He saw it and wasted no time spinning around on the cruiser and letting the bullets fly. He let off several shots that went through the windshield. The two officers fell out of the cruiser, and Spring peeled off, hitting Vick's car in the process. He spun back around and let off a few rounds at her car.

"Get down! Get down!" Spring yelled as she maneuvered the Chrysler 300 through the intersection into moving traffic.

A bullet hit Vick on top of his left shoulder and almost knocked him to the ground. He spun back around to the cops and let off another round of bullets, that time hitting one of the cops in the chest. Vick backed up to his car, all the while continuing to fire upon the officers. He managed to get in his car and pull off. The unwounded officer fired several shots at Vick but didn't hit him. He immediately got on his radio and gave dispatch a description of Vick's car.

Homicide detectives and uniformed cops crawled all over Mike's shop. The Cane Corso had viciously dismembered the female's small body. Her breast had been ripped off and her neck was halfway chewed through. The dog had done so much damage to the young female's face that she was unrecognizable.

"What do you have in here?" Detective Keys asked when he walked into the shop where his partner was.

"I don't think this is a regular body shop," Detective Allen said. He rose up from behind the counter and placed several small pouches onto the counter. He emptied out one of them, which contained four Rolex watches. The other pouches revealed more pieces of jewelry such as custom-made chains, diamond rings, and a couple of diamond bracelets.

"Rolex," Detective Keys said. He held one of the watches up in the air. Just out of curiosity, he dug into his back pocket and pulled out his notepad. He wanted to see if the serial numbers matched the ones from the empty case at Mac's house.

"Son of a bitch," he blurted out when he saw that the numbers matched.

A commotion outside of the shop caught Keys's attention before he could tell his partner about the serial number.

"What the hell is going on?" he asked when he looked outside.

Uniformed cops were rushing to their cars, causing Keys to turn up the volume on his own radio.

"Shots fired! Shots fired! Officer down! Officer down!" the dispatcher yelled into the radio.

"Stay here, I got it," Keys told his partner as he headed for the door. He yelled over his shoulder, before he took off to join the pursuit with the rest of the law enforcement, "Make sure you bag and tag that jewelry!"

Spring brought her car to a slow stop at Orange Storage Company, right off Christian Street on the west side. Aside from the few bullet holes in her trunk and a shattered back window, she and Corey were fine.

"This nigga musta lost his mind!" Spring said and hit the steering wheel with both hands.

When she got out of the car to assess the damage, she let out a sigh. "I told Trey that nigga was a piece of shit." She paced back and forth. "Something has always been off about him."

Corey didn't say a word. He didn't need to. From the moment that Vick had pulled a gun out on them, he'd already made his bed. Then he'd actually busted at them. Corey was going to kill him.

Corey pulled out his phone, and just for kicks, he dialed Vick's number. He really just wanted to see if Vick had been locked up or shot dead by the police. Unexpectedly, Vick answered the phone.

"Save me the song and the dance about how you gon' kill me," Vick said as he sat on the bus looking out the window at all the cop cars darting in the opposite direction. Shortly after the shootout, he'd abandoned his car and jumped on public transportation.

"Nah, bro, I'm not gonna tell you what you already know," Corey replied.

"Is that him? Is that him?" Spring exclaimed. She came around the car and snatched the phone from Corey's ear. "You gon' shoot at me, though? You greedy muthafucka."

"Bitch, I take money. That's what I do. You the only one who seem to be forgetting who we are!" Vick replied calmly.

"That was part of the setup, you stupid asshole!"

Vick hung up the phone on her, not wanting to hear what she had to say.

Spring knew going back and forth wasn't going to get either of them anywhere. In her mind, Vick was an idiot who had almost just messed everything up for them. He'd let his anger cloud his judgment. All of his money was tied up with Spring, and he'd just made her his enemy. He was broke and alone, and that is how Spring knew he had a couple more tricks up his sleeve.

"I gotta get this dope to Mike before he has a heart attack," Spring said. She opened the back door and grabbed the duffle bag so she could transfer it to the Range Rover. "Look, take this car back to the garage, and then meet me at—"

Corey looked at Spring like she was crazy. "We're not splitting up. We can leave this car right here in storage and stay together," he told her.

After some thought, Spring agreed, feeling like she might be a little safer with Corey close by. Now, all she had to do was get Summer out of harm's way, at least until all of the craziness was over.

Spring drove down the street where Mike's auto body shop was. She almost shitted on herself when she saw a few police cars and yellow tape wrapped around the front entrance of the shop.

"That's a homicide," Corey announced.

Spring parked her car down the street. She had to see what was going on since she was in possession of the heroin. Corey got out of the car and followed her.

"Excuse me, what happened over here?" Spring asked a young Puerto Rican female who was standing across the street with a crowd of spectators.

"Somebody done killed Mike, and some girl got ate up by that big-ass dog," she reported.

Spring looked over at Corey with confusion written all over her face. Not needing to hear anything else, Spring walked off from the scene.

"Do you think . . ." Spring stopped midsentence and thought about what she was about to say. "Do you think Vick had something to do with this?" she asked Corey as they walked toward the car.

Before Corey could answer her question, Spring's phone began to vibrate in her pocket. Vick's number popped up on the screen.

"Is this ya work?" she asked.

Vick chuckled. "Yeah, I'm just now seeing this shit on the news. It's fucked up what happened to my li'l bitch, though. She had potential."

"Vick, you are a real piece of shit."

"I told you we might as well have just kept the dope. I been planning this shit ever since you agreed to do the drop. I told you before that I'm a taker. You better get that shit through ya head."

Vick had figured that Spring wasn't going to comply with what he was on, so her head along with Corey's head were now on the chopping block.

"Last chance to make it right," Vick offered. He got up from his seat and walked into the dining room. "The hard work is done already," he said.

"Vick, do you really think that his people are going to forget about their dope?" Spring asked. She couldn't believe that Vick hadn't thought any of his actions through all the way to the end. That much product would make anybody come look for you. Mike's family wasn't just coming for the dope; they were going to want the head of whoever was responsible for killing Mike. Spring wasn't ready to go to war, especially for something that she didn't do.

"A'ight, fuck you then. I'll settle for this gift that you left here for me at the spot." Vick spoke of the money that they were supposed to use for the sting with Gary. "Don't worry. By the time you get here, I'll be gone."

Spring was sick. That was everything that she had to her name. "I hope it was all worth it. When I see you, I'ma kill you. Painfully," Spring said before she hung up the phone.

Before Spring could even attempt to catch up with Vick, she had to get the bag full of dope out the back seat out of her car and to its rightful owner, and pray that they didn't think she had something to do with Mike's death.

"Come on, let's get out of here," Spring said.

"Mom, don't be like that," Summer said as she gave herself a tour of her sister's house. "I'll be over there in the morning and we can go get our nails and feet done."

"Yeah, 'cause I didn't go all the way up to your college to get you just so you can be with that crazy sister of yours," Ms. Gloria shot back. "I want some time too! You make sure that you have ya ass over here first thing in the morning or it's going to be a problem."

Summer chuckled at her mother. "Mom, I'll be there in the morning," she assured her before ending the call.

No more than two seconds went by before Summer's phone rang. "I know you're not gonna leave me in this house all night," Summer answered. She already knew it was Spring by the ringtone. Spring had a nice house, but Summer was already starting to get bored.

"I know, sis. I'm sorry. It's a lot of drama going on right now and I just need for you to stay put until this stuff dies down."

"Hell, I'm about to take my ass back over Mama's house."

"Look, I'ma be there in a couple of hours, I promise. Until then, just please relax ya'self," Spring said as she watched Corey pump gas into the car.

"Well, can you at least bring Mama up here wit' you? We were supposed to have Sunday dinner at her house. Matter of fact, why don't we just do it here?" Summer suggested.

Spring thought about it and dinner did sound like the perfect idea. That meant Summer and her mom would be in a safe place. Spring knew and understood how vicious the streets could be. She also knew that she didn't want her loved ones in the line of fire.

"Okay, I'll pick Mama up and bring her with me. I'll talk to you soon," Spring said then hung up.

Chapter 7

"I'm telling you, amigo, it had to be a hit," Santana said to a few of Mike's family members as they sat around in the family restaurant. "I have a feeling that bitch Spring had something to do with this shit. And she still has the dope."

Benny, Mike's older brother and the rightful owner of the dope, listened as Santana explained his theory about what had happened. Benny didn't know Spring personally, but from what Mike had told him about her she didn't sound like the type who would do something like that. However, he didn't put anything past anyone when it came to money and the streets. Until he had the chance to speak to her, a clear understanding wasn't going to be reached.

"A'ight, put some guys out on the streets and see if we can get a location on this chick." Before he could get another word out, the front door of the restaurant swung open, and in walked Vick.

"Whoa, whoa," one of Benny's guys said, sticking his hands out to stop Vick.

"Yo, tell Benny I need to holla at him," Vick said as he was being patted down. A .357 Sig was removed from his waist immediately.

"Tell him I know where his dope is," Vick said loud enough so Benny and everybody else in the back could hear him.

Benny instantly got out of his seat and walked to the front. "Vick, it's been awhile since I saw you."

"Yeah, I know. I been on some low-key shit lately. But check this out. Let me put you up on game about ya shit."

"Speak." Benny was all ears.

"Word on the street is the chick robbed ya folks. I used to do some business with her, so I know a sting for some dope is right up her alley," Vick said. "She's vicious like that, and I know from experience. Shit, I think I might even know where she's hiding it."

"I told you that bitch was foul," Santana mumbled as he stood behind Benny.

Benny was hesitant to believe Vick because it was a catch twenty-two when it came to men like him. Benny had been in the streets too long to think anything different. "So, you're telling me all of this because of what?" Benny asked.

Vick's lies poured out like they were the actual truth. "Man, that bitch robbed me for a hundred thousand. I'm hoping that if I help you find the dope, you'll cut a nigga a check," Vick replied.

Benny looked at Santana and then back at Vick. He knew there was something fishy going on, but Benny didn't care. There was a million dollars' worth of heroin at stake, so a finder's fee was better than not getting any of it back at all.

"A'ight. If you find my shit, I'll give you 50K," Benny told him.

Vick accepted his offer without hesitation. He definitely already had an idea where the dope was. The only problem he had was getting a couple of guys to help him get to it. Benny didn't have a problem accommodating him with two boys from his own crew. It wasn't much, but it was all Vick figured he needed for the task at hand.

Spring, Summer, and Ms. Gloria sat in the nail salon getting the works: manicure, pedicure, and mud facials. Spring wasn't going to come, but Ms. Gloria wasn't having it. Since they all agreed to go out for dinner instead of staying in, Ms. Gloria decided to make it a full-blown girls' day out.

"You better not dare get on that phone," Ms. Gloria looked over and told Spring, who had pulled her phone out of her bag. "I just want to enjoy a couple of hours with my girls without any interruptions!"

"Yeah, I'm going back to school tonight, so let's just chill," Summer chimed in.

They just didn't understand what Spring had on her plate but, in a sense, Spring was glad that they didn't. She put her phone back into her bag, not wanting to be the one who ruined the day. As she sat there and actively participated in the activities, Spring couldn't help but to think about what she was going to do with the heroin. She knew of Mike's brother, but she didn't have a number for him and she didn't want to just go around his neighborhood asking for him. She knew that it was only going to be a matter of time before Mike's people came looking for her. Fortunately for her, there was one person she could go to, to get in contact with Mike's people. All she had to do was get through the day, which now only consisted of having dinner and dropping Summer back off to her school. After that, it was yard out.

Corey eased his way through the door of the apartment, not completely sure if Vick was in there. He had his gun in hand, down by his side, as he slowly walked through the apartment. When he got up to the china cabinet, it was obvious that the stash had been hit. Even with it being a little more than $100,000, Corey knew that Vick wasn't going to go far with it at all. He blew money just as fast as he got it. Another thing working against

Vick was his greed; he never had enough. Corey was going to count on that poor quality to lead him straight to Vick. He was going to expose himself eventually and, when he did, Corey was going to be all over him like flies on trash.

"I'ma blow ya fuckin head off, boy," Corey mumbled to himself then headed for the front door.

Detective Keys walked into the small conference room toting his leather satchel over his shoulder. Detective Allen and two other detectives were already in the room going over the notes. Two homicides were being investigated at the same time because they seemed to be connected: the one in Mac's house and the one at the body shop. The evidence of two of Mac's Rolex watches being in the shop along with several other pieces of jewelry linked the two cases together. The detectives didn't know if it was just a coincidence that Mac's jewelry had ended up in the body shop, but they weren't about to sign off on that notion until they were 100 percent sure of it.

"The DNA came in this morning," Detective Allen said, passing Keys the folder. "There were traces of Mac's, of course. And there was also a woman's discharge on Mac's penis and on the sheets. The discharge was pretty much dried up, so the sexual intercourse had to have taken place the night before."

"Did we run it through our database to see if we got a hit?" Keys asked while he read the results.

"I have Pam running it through the system as we speak. If the female has ever been incarcerated, we will get a hit. Oh, and we also have some footage from the ATM machine that was across the street from the body shop. There had been a significant amount of traffic going in and out of the shop before the murder. Whenever you're ready, we can go and take a look at it," one of the other detectives spoke up.

Keys closed the folder and sat back in his chair, delving into deep thought. He was trying to think of a way that these two cases could have been linked together, but it was still a little too early in the investigation to come up with a good scenario.

"If I don't know anything else, I know somebody else was in the room when Mac and Trey were murdered. More than likely, whoever that person was brought some of that jewelry down to Mike's to pawn it off," said Keys.

"Yeah, and the DNA didn't add up to the female who was gnawed by that dog, so that rules her out," Allen added. "Feel like we just hit another brick wall."

Although the case had just gotten started, Keys was already becoming frustrated. Until something else revealed itself, the detective was almost at a standstill. Of course, Keys still had a couple more tricks up his sleeve. He knew he just needed to get out and hit the streets. He began to pack up his things, looking around the room at his colleagues.

"I guess it's time we do it the old-fashioned way," he said then got up from his seat. "We go knock on a couple of doors."

All the detectives followed suit and were up and out the door right behind Detective Keys.

"Damn, *papis*, y'all don't know how to pick a lock?" Vick said to both of the Spanish guys as they stood on Ms. Gloria's front porch. The sun was almost set, so most of the neighbors had gone inside for the night. "Watch out."

Vick moved them away from the front door. He didn't know how to pick a lock either, but he was a pro at shoulder bumping somebody's door open. The thump wasn't even that loud and, just like that, he was inside. One of the Spanish guys followed him into the house while the other stood outside.

"Check down here," Vick instructed as he took to the steps.

Vick hit every room, flipping beds, ripping up carpets, and emptying out drawers. All three rooms including the bathroom and the hallway closet were mangled within minutes. The Spanish guy downstairs didn't find anything either. A quick sweep of the basement came up empty, and Vick knew if the dope wasn't there then there was only one other place it could be. He knew Spring like a book, and he had no doubt that she would keep it somewhere safe and somewhat secured.

"Come on, let's get the fuck out of here," Vick said as he headed to the front door.

His next destination was the Orange Storage Company.

Spring looked in her rearview mirror at her mother asleep in the back seat.

"Here, this is for you." Spring went into the center console, pulled out a wad of money, and passed it to Summer. "I know college can be a little expensive." She glanced over at her sister with a smile on her face. "Before you even ask, it's twenty grand that I been holding on to for a while."

Summer leaned over and gave her sister a kiss on the cheek. If she could count on anybody to hold her down, it was Spring. Things did get expensive at UNC, and that wasn't even including tuition. The twenty grand would go a long way.

"Look at my two girls," a groggy voice said from the back seat. Ms. Gloria woke up right on time because the college was up ahead.

"So when will we see you again?" Spring asked as she pulled off on the exit.

"I don't know. I got a final exam coming up in one of my classes, and then we got this other thing popping off."

"Well, go ahead and do ya thing then," Spring said. "Whenever you're ready to come home for a few days, I'll come and pick you up."

"Please don't make me come back up here, 'cause you know I will." Ms. Gloria chuckled.

The student parking lot came up too fast, and after lots of hugs, kisses, and a few tears, Summer got her things and headed back to school. It was emotional for Spring. Any time she and her twin separated it was like a part of her was ripped away. A piece of her had left with Summer, and until she came back home again, that slot would remain vacant.

Vick and the two Spanish guys pulled up in front of the Orange Storage Company just as night fell. Vick knew about the two security guards who worked the night shift and how one would stay in the booth while the other patrolled the storage units. They were only armed with Taser guns, something that they would second-guess pulling out once they saw real guns.

"You hold down the mafucka in the booth, and you? You come with me," Vick directed.

The Spanish kid did exactly what he was told and headed straight to the booth while Vick and his partner went around the back way.

Vick cut through the gate with a pair of bolt cutters then slightly jogged around the east wing of the units. Each unit was large enough to store a car in it, and on many occasions Vick had witnessed Spring putting her vehicles in there.

"Here it is right over here." Vick pointed to the number 215 over the door.

Vick looked around before taking the tool and popping the lock off. When he lifted the gate, it was just as he expected. The shot-up Chrysler 300 was inside. Once he finally popped the trunk open, he knew that he'd hit the jackpot. The duffle bag of heroin was sitting right there.

"Come check it out," Vick said, waving the Spanish guy over.

He walked over, reached in, and unzipped the bag, then pulled out one of the bricks of heroin with a smile on his face. The Spanish guy's happiness wouldn't last long. Vick had his gun out and aimed right at his head. The Spanish guy never saw a thing. Only a bright flash before everything went dark.

Vick threw the duffel bag over his shoulder and walked out of the unit, but not before closing the gate behind him. Instead of going out the same way that he came in, Vick took the bandana out of his back pocket, wrapped it around his face, and walked toward the booth. The guard patrolling the units thought he heard a gunshot and had gone over to the east wing to check on it.

The other Spanish guy was in the booth holding the second guard at gunpoint.

"Yo, let's get out of here," Vick said when he walked up and tapped the window.

As soon as the guy opened the door to the booth, Vick hit him. Pop! A single bullet hit him in his chest, dropping him to the ground.

Vick stood over him and shot him several more times. The guard was scared to death and just knew that he was about to get it next, but Vick didn't shoot him. He simply disappeared into the night.

Wanting to spend a little more time with her daughter, Ms. Gloria decided to spend the night at Spring's house. Spring couldn't deny her even if she wanted to.

"A'ight, Mama, I gotta go take care of a few things, but I'll be back in about an hour," she told her mom once she got her settled into the home.

The only thing Spring had on her mind was going down to Puerto Rican land off of Central Avenue to find her girlfriend, Rosa. She pretty much knew everybody who was somebody in that neighborhood. If there was anyone who could help find Mike's brother it was her.

"Let me see where this nigga at," Spring mumbled to herself. She pulled out her phone to call Corey.

"What?" he answered his phone with an attitude.

Spring smiled. She knew that he had been worrying about her and it felt kind of good. "Boy, you better watch ya tone answering the phone like that."

"Where the fuck were you at, Spring?" He sounded like he had been chewing something. "You haven't answered ya phone all fucking day."

Spring bit down on her lower lip. He sounded sexy when he was mad. Honestly, that was one of the things that turned her on about him. But now wasn't the time for all that.

"I'm on my way to the north side so I can try to make contact with Mike's folks. You think you can meet me on Fifth and Giraud in like an hour?"

Corey was in his feelings about her being MIA all day, but he was always on call whenever Spring needed him. All she had to do was ask. "You crazy as hell. I'll see you in an hour."

It took a minute, but when Spring finally got back into the city, the first thing she did was hit Rosa up. Her neighborhood was probably the most violent in the city, so Spring made sure she kept her strap on her. When she pulled up to Pike Street there were so many people out there, mainly dopefiends. Instead of parking on the block, Spring spun around the corner and got out to walk. The Glock 9 mm was tucked snug in her back pocket.

"*Hola, mami,*" Rosa greeted her. She came down the steps to give Spring a hug. A couple of dope boys stood around, doing what they did.

"Damn, girl, I haven't been down here in a minute, but from the looks of it, y'all still getting a lot of money," Spring said, looking up and down the street at all the traffic. Rosa's block was one of the few left in the city that sold large amounts of heroin.

"So, look, I'm trying to get in contact with Mike's people. It's an emergency," Spring said.

"I know them, but them muthafuckas is crazy, *mami*."

"Not as crazy as me." Spring laughed, trying to make a joke out of it.

Rosa smiled. "You right about that. But I think his brother owns a restaurant over on D and Cambria. I think his—"

"Yo, one time!" one of the block workers yelled out. "They comin' in hot!" he yelled, seeing several police cars racing down the block.

He along with several other people took off running from the gate. They knew what it was. Spring looked up and saw everybody scatter like roaches.

"Just walk with me," Rosa instructed Spring in a calm voice as she started down the street.

Cops were coming from every direction and, for a minute, Spring thought they were about to fall from the sky.

"Just keep walking. Look normal," Rosa advised her.

The girls were just approaching the corner when, out of nowhere, an unmarked car drove up on the sidewalk, cutting them off.

"Don't move. Let me see ya hands," the narcotics detective yelled out as he drew his weapon.

The raid was unexpected and happened so fast that Spring forgot she had the Glock 9 mm in her back pocket. It was the first thing the detective noticed when he saw her, and the ultimate reason he stopped them. Spring thought about running when she finally realized that she had the gun on her. But by that time it was too late. Several other police officers were right up on her. After recovering the gun, Spring and Rosa were taken into custody without further incident.

Corey sat in his car on Fifth and Giraud, waiting for Spring to show. It was only after she was about half an hour late that he decided to call her phone. It just kept ringing and ringing, and when she didn't answer, Corey called right back. Finally, somebody did answer, but it wasn't Spring.

"Hello?" a female voice said from the other end.

Chapter 8

Detective Keys walked out of the storage unit with his phone to his ear. He looked back and watched as the forensics unit took pictures of the body and collected pieces of evidence.

"I need to put an APB out on a female named Spring Stewart. Last known address: 1503 Covecreek Drive," Keys told his partner, who was still at the station finishing up some paperwork.

"Hold on, let me run this through Pam," Allen replied.

Detective Keys stayed on the line explaining some of the detail of the double homicide he'd run into on his way to work. The case had two homicide detectives working it, but Keys wanted to help out as much as he could. The first twenty-four hours were critical in a murder case.

"You're not gonna believe this," Detective Allen said. "She's here. The girl you asked about is here right now."

"Get the hell out of here!" Keys said incredulously. "Don't let her leave."

"She's not going anywhere. Narcs picked her up last night for a gun possession," Allen said.

Spring and Rosa were still waiting to see the judge so they could post bail, and in that district it could take anywhere from twelve to twenty-four hours to be seen. That was more than enough time for the detective to get down to the station and have a few words with her. The rental car was in her name and so was the storage unit. She would have to answer questions regarding that and also explain the multiple bullet holes in the car. There were too many questions, and for some reason, Detective Keys knew that she held all of the answers.

Vick took in a deep pull of the blunt and then exhaled the thick white smoke into the air. His weed was potent and had his whole motel room foggy as ever. He looked over at the duffle bag of heroin sitting on the bed, and although he had come up on over a million dollars, he knew it was far from over. Loose ends needed to be tied up and it was time to get the ball rolling. Vick's cell phone ringing snapped him out of his train of thought. When he looked and saw who it was, he wasn't surprised at all; it was a call he'd been waiting for all morning.

"Yo, what up, Benny?" He took another pull of the weed.

Benny was pissed off after seeing what happened at the storage company on the news that morning. "You better have my fuckin' dope," Benny said from the other end of the phone.

"Man, the bitch was waiting for us. It was a setup," Vick lied. "I got hit too. I'm on my way to the hospital right now."

Vick blamed everything on Spring, only making Benny angrier. It was getting to the point where he wanted to say fuck the dope and kill everyone involved, and that included Vick.

"Find my dope or find me the bitch. Or else, I'm going to do it myself. And if I do it myself, nobody is safe," Benny said then hung up the phone.

Vick sat there thinking about how in the world he could deliver Spring without getting himself killed in the process. The thought of simply taking off with what he had came to Vick's mind, but with both Spring and her crew along with Benny and his looking for him, he figured there weren't too many places he could go in North Carolina or South Carolina. Besides, he really didn't want to leave the city. He loved his hood, but the only way he was going to be able to stay and live comfortably was if he came up with a way to neutralize the beef he had with Spring and Corey, and now Benny as well.

"This must be ya first time being locked up, huh?" Rosa observed as she lay down on the bench in the back of the holding cell.

"Yeah, how can you tell?" Spring asked.

Rosa started laughing. "'Cause your ass has been standing up by the door for the last six hours." She continued to chuckle. "This process takes forever. The good thing is we should be seeing the judge in a couple of hours."

It definitely wasn't Rosa's first time being locked up, so she was quite familiar with the process. She had already done a two-year stretch in a women's state prison. With her still being on probation for her last case, she would be lucky if she even got bail.

"Stewart!" an officer yelled and almost walked past her cell.

Spring waved her hand to stop him. "I'm right here."

"Okay, it's time to get this show on the road," Rosa said and sat up on the bench. She figured it wouldn't be long before they called her name.

The officer unlocked the door and let Spring out then handcuffed her immediately. She heard the sound of his keys clanking together when he locked the cell behind her, and she felt his hand on her elbow. He led her down the hallway and upstairs. Spring assumed she was being taken to the courtroom, but instead they ended up in the homicide unit.

"I got her," a tall white man in a suit said once he saw the two enter.

His hand on her arm replaced the officer's and he took over. All eyes were on Spring and it made her uneasy. A part of her wished she could run, but another part wanted to curse everyone out for looking at her like she was an exhibit at the zoo. Next, she was taken to an interrogation room and was forced to take a seat at a wooden table.

"What's going on?" she asked once she was seated.

Before she could receive an answer Detective Allen and Detective Keys walked into the room and Spring began to wonder what was really going on. Both men took a seat on the other side of the table and eyed her curiously.

"Hello, Ms. Stewart, my name is Detective Keys and this here is Detective Allen. We are currently working a homicide case. A couple actually."

"Homicide?" Spring tried to make her face as blank as possible. "Then why am I here? I ain't kill nobody."

The detectives looked at each other briefly and then back at Spring, already knowing that she was hiding something.

"Nobody is saying that you did. But what I find funny is that somehow your name is linked to every case we are working, so I'm assuming you're going to tell me that is just a coincidence, right?"

"Must be," Spring said without missing a beat.

"Let me ask you this, Ms. Stewart. Where is the car you just rented from Dollar Rentals?" Detective Allen adjusted the ink pen in his hand and got ready to write down everything she uttered.

Spring knew that if he was asking a question, then more than likely he already knew the answer. "I rented a Chrysler 300 the other day and it got shot up pretty bad by some lunatic who was trying to carjack me. But the police came and the crazy-ass nigga started shooting at them. I got the hell out of there. I put the car in the storage unit until it was time for me to take it back. Why, what's going on?" Spring asked, switching the focus.

"There were two murders that took place in the storage unit. And your unit was the only one open. Was there anything in the car that was of value? Something that somebody may have wanted?" Allen asked.

"I only had the car in my possession for a couple of hours before the attempted carjack. That was the reason I had the gun on me, for protection," Spring replied.

Everything that Spring said sounded authentic, and it even gave a little clarity on how the cop shooting on Washington Avenue went down. However, Detective Allen couldn't understand why Spring didn't just call the cops and report the shooting. That alone made it seem like she was hiding something or protecting someone. As soon as the detective was about to dig deeper into her story, the interview room door opened. It was their supervisor, Parker, telling them to step into the hallway so that he could have a word with them.

"I think I'm on to something," Allen said in a hushed tone.

"Well, whatever it is, it's going to have to wait because that girl has a lawyer," Parker said. He nodded in the direction of Jack McMan, a well-known lawyer in the city.

"Just five more minutes," Keys pleaded. "I think she knows more than she's letting on."

The supervisor shook his head. McMan wasn't the type of lawyer who could be played around with. Not only was he a criminal lawyer, but his wife was the best civil lawyer in the city, and she had made a name for herself by suing the police numerous times. The police department didn't need those types of problems, and for that reason the interview was officially over for now, and probably forever.

Ms. Gloria slowly walked through her house, stepping over debris that was scattered about. It looked like a tornado had hit it. Her whole body shook and her eyes were open wide. Her confusion level was at its peak because she had no idea who would come and do something like that. She pulled out her phone and attempted to call the cops, but when she walked into the kitchen, her heart almost fell out of her chest. A man she didn't recognize was standing there leaning against the sink with a gun in his hand.

"Put the phone on the table," he instructed Ms. Gloria.

She was scared out her mind, but had enough sense to comply. "I don't have any money," she said. "Please don't hurt me."

"I'm not here to hurt you. I just want you to deliver this message to your daughter. Tell her to get me what belongs to me, or else I will kill you and everything else she loves. Do you understand?" Benny threatened. "And if the cops are contacted, I will be sure to make the deaths long and painful."

Ms. Gloria was terrified, but still she nodded her head.

The man started to make his exit from the kitchen. When he got next to her, he stopped and she didn't even want to look at him.

"Tell your daughter Benny was here," he added, then walked off, leaving Ms. Gloria frozen.

The only reason he didn't shoot her right then was because he didn't want to lose his leverage in the situation. The conversation with Spring's mother was sure to get her attention in every way that he wanted it. Benny was about his business, and the last thing he planned to do was take a million-dollar loss on top of losing his brother. Something had to give.

Fats, Chill, and Rob stood in the middle of the block doing what they did best: trapping. Chill was the first to notice a guy coming down the street with a black hood over his head. Fats turned his head and saw the same, prompting him to pull the .45 from his waistline. Corey pulled the hood from over his head right as Fats was about to shoot.

"Nigga, you was about to be on the ground leaking," Fats said and tucked his gun back into his pocket.

Corey walked up and gave everybody dap. It had a been awhile since he had to trap out there, but his face was still good with his people.

"My bad. Ay, did any of y'all see that nigga, Vick?" Corey asked. Corey and Vick had grown up in the same hood, so they pretty much knew the same people, but quiet as kept, everybody liked Corey more than they liked Vick.

"Yeah, that nigga came around here earlier, talking about he had some diesel for sale. He said he had it for the low, too. So you know I wasn't trying to buy none of that shit." Chill laughed.

"You know that nigga stay scheming," Fats said and then noticed the way Corey's jaw was clenched. "Damn, you got that look in ya eyes. What, y'all niggas beefin' about something?"

"Yeah, something like that," Corey answered. "Look, if that nigga come back through here, call my phone."

He dished a round of parting daps and then left. Words didn't even have to be said for Fats to know that some shit was about to go down between those two. Because Vick was just as much of a killer as Corey, Fats was going to stay out of it.

It was nightfall by the time Ms. Gloria came through with bail money for both Spring and Rosa.

"Girl, just come to the block whenever so I can give you ya money back," Rosa said as they stood in front of the police station.

"Girl, I'm not coming back down on that block. The next time I come visit you, ya ass gon' have to meet me somewhere." Spring laughed and gave Rosa a hug.

"A'ight, *mami,* I'll catch you around," Rosa said when her ride pulled up. And then she was gone.

"Thank you, Mom," Spring said to her mother as they walked toward the parking lot. "I really appreciate—"

"Thank you, my ass. What in the world is going on wit' you? Is this the way you really wanna live ya life?" Ms. Gloria began to cry, thinking about the message Benny had told her to give Spring.

"Mom, it's okay. You don't have to cry."

"Some man came by my house and trashed it. He was waiting for me to come home. Oh, God, I was so scared!" Ms. Gloria cried out. "He threatened to kill both me and you if you didn't give him whatever it is of his that you have. What did you do? What the fuck did you do, Spring?" Tears poured out of Ms. Gloria's eyes and they did exactly what she thought they would do.

"Somebody broke into your house, Mama?" Spring was alarmed. "What did he look like?"

"He was a Spanish man with a heavy accent."

"Did he tell you his name or leave a number?"

"He said his name was Benny. And that you have something that belongs to him. Spring, I don't want to lose you! You need to just go on 'head and give him what he wants and leave this mess behind you!" Ms. Gloria said.

Spring wrapped her mother up in her arms, hating to see her like this. "You aren't going to lose me. I want you to stay at my house until I take care of this. Trust me, Mom, nothing is going to happen to me. This is all just one big misunderstanding," Spring assured her.

Spring had to admit the news about the double homicide at the storage facility was a shock, and the fact that the dope was gone created another problem. Problems she didn't know if she was going to be able to handle. She had an idea of who could have taken it, but until she got back on the streets, she wasn't going to know for sure. Getting her mother somewhere safe was the top priority.

"I want a tail on her twenty-four seven. That girl is the leading key to this case," Parker barked out. "I want a ballistics report on that gun she had in her possession. And I wanna know why was she on Pike Street at night with a firearm on her anyway. I want to know everything about this girl by the end of the night!"

"So, does this mean I get to work some overtime?" Allen joked.

Little did he know, he and every detective working the case were about to get plenty of overtime. Not just one, but two people were dead, along with an officer in critical condition. The case was a serious one and nobody was going to sleep until something was figured out.

Now that Parker was on to Spring, there was no way he was going to let up until he was sure that she had nothing to do with any of the incidents.

Chapter 9

Trey was something like a celebrity in the hood, so it only made sense that his funeral was a celebration. Everybody came through to see him off, and out of the couple hundred people who showed up, there were only a few somber faces in the place. The spirit that everyone had was only a reflection of how Trey had treated them when he was home.

"Lord knows he wasn't a saint when it came to the streets, but he had a good heart," Trey's mother, Ms. Gladice, said from the podium. "He took care of so many people, and if he couldn't give you money, he'd give you some advice that was worth the same or maybe even more."

Everybody in the church was quiet as they listened, but they nodded their heads in agreement.

Spring sat in the front row listening to it all. Tears fell from under her Gucci shades, and the only thing she could think about was how much she wished Trey was alive. The advice from everybody thus far was for her to be strong, but with all that was going on with her, she didn't even know how that could be possible. She was on edge. Each moment she spent sitting still was another second shaved off her life. She was so deep into the service that she didn't even know that Corey had come and taken a seat next to her.

"I need to holla at you for a minute," Corey leaned in and whispered in Spring's ear.

She nodded then got up and followed him off to the side.

"Those people are outside right now."

"What people?" Spring asked.

They walked toward the front of the church. Spring's temper flared. For anybody to bring drama to Trey's funeral was like flirting with death. The FNS .40-cal that had been in her bag was removed and strapped to her thigh under her black dress. When she got outside, she saw exactly what Corey was talking about. Parked right outside like the mob were three all-black Mercedes-Benzes. One man stood out. He leaned on the side of his shiny car and gazed at her from behind the dark tint of his designer sunglasses. Draped on his body was a Tom Ford two-button suit and on his face was a smile.

"I bet anything that you're Spring," he said as she made her way down the church steps. The .40-cal slightly bulged out on her thigh. That made Benny smile.

"Yeah, I'm her, and I already know who you are. You're the one who trashed my mother's house. Didn't your mother teach you any manners, nigga?" she snapped back with plenty of attitude.

"You're correct." Benny chuckled. "My name is Benny, Mike's brother. I'm just simply trying to collect what is rightfully mine, and then I will be on my way."

"I hate to be the one to tell you this, but I don't have ya dope. The same person who killed ya brother—"

"I don't think you want to play that game with me, pretty girl," Benny interrupted. "Let's not make things get ugly out here."

Spring's heart began to race when she saw a police cruiser bend the corner and drive slowly in their direction. Benny turned his head and shook it when he saw what she was staring at. The car parked not too far away from the church.

"Don't think that's gon' stop me from shooting this muthafuckin' funeral up. I don't give a fuck who's around," Benny told her.

"By the way, your mother seems like a real nice lady," he said as a sly smile crept across his face.

"Don't you dare say shit about my mother," Spring said through her teeth.

His comment had Spring so mad that she started to reach for her gun. Out of nowhere, another cop car drove down the block and parked even closer to the church. Spring eased up and so did Corey, who was also ready to let bullets fly. One cop car really didn't make a difference, but two of them had Benny thinking twice.

"I'll see you in traffic, and the next time we cross paths, you better have my shit. You got lucky this time," Benny said with a wink.

He waved to his boys, and just like that they all got into their cars and pulled off. Spring got a good look at all three of their cars as they drove away, and once they were out of sight, she and Corey headed back into the church.

"Yo, Fats, let me holla at you," Vick yelled from up the street.

When Fats turned around and saw who it was, the first person who came to mind was Corey. "Damn, playboy, what it look like?" Fats gave Vick some dap.

Vick's sales pitch kicked in immediately. He let it be known that he had some good dope for the low, much like what Chill had told them the other night. Vick even pulled out a sample bag and told Fats to give it to one of his customers, which he did, just to see what it was hitting for.

"Damn, so what's up wit' you and Corey? Word on the streets is that y'all two niggas is beefin'," Fats said as they waited on the junkie to do his thing. "You know we all boys. There's no need for us to be going to war with each other. We need to be tryin' to get this money together."

"Yeah, I know, but you know how it is when a nigga is coming up in the game. Everybody wanna bring you down," Vick replied. He looked around with his hand in his pocket, wrapped around a gun. Just the mention of Corey's name had him paranoid.

"Damn, check dis shit out," Vick said. He pointed to the dopefiend sitting on the steps with his head in his lap after instantly feeling the dope he'd just shot in his arm. "See, that's what I'm talking about."

He ran down the prices to Fats, which were lower than all the other prices in the city. Vick was almost giving it away. A true hustler could tell that he was just trying to get it off. One thing that Fats knew was that he had done something foul to Corey, but prices like this were hard to come by. Fats wanted in on it. Regardless of any beef, he had to eat, and he'd just come across a come up. It was something he would have to just charge to the game. Fats was only trying to capitalize off a messed-up situation.

Corey had to call a few of his boys to come down to the church just so they could have a few more guns on deck. Spring couldn't say that he was dragging it out, either. Benny had confronted her in broad daylight, and she knew the only thing that had saved her from having a bullet between her eyes was the fact that the police had shown up.

Spring knew things were getting heavy and she needed to make moves fast. Vick had to be stopped at all costs. She had a couple of soldiers on deck, ready to put in some work if need be. She knew when violence was necessary, and how much to apply.

"So, how do you wanna handle this?" Corey asked as Spring watched Trey's casket come down the steps.

Vick's stupidity and greed had put everybody in a messed-up situation. She didn't have too many options to choose from. Either she could find Vick and get the dope back, or she would have to go to war with Benny and his people.

"I want to try one more thing before shit hits the fan," Spring replied. "I have to have a sit-down with Gary. We need to get this money. It's the only way we can nip this in the bud."

"Nah, it's another way. We can go up north and smoke them niggas. We not duckin' no rec," Corey said.

"Nah, Corey. I got too many eyes on me. The feds are on to all of this shit, so we have to be smart. We can't just go guns blazing at anybody. War just leads to more war. Before I go and put other people's lives in jeopardy, I wanna try and handle this another way. It was our people who fucked up. We put our trust in the wrong nigga. Vick had done some bullshit, but at the end of the day, he was a part of this crew. I'ma try to make it right first. If that don't work, we'll just do what we have to do," Spring told him.

Corey knew where she was coming from, but he needed the world to know that there was no bitch in his blood. He was ready to go round for round. If it were up to him, he'd take twenty soldiers up north with him and shoot anybody with a Spanish accent, just for being disrespectful. That's how hard he was willing to go, especially for Spring. He'd take a bullet for her without question.

Detective Keys took his glasses off and wiped the corner of his eyes. Overtime was an understatement, and ever since Parker had said his piece the other day, Keys had been working his ass off. With having multiple cases to work, he didn't see any free time in his near future. It was a good thing that he wasn't married because he definitely would have been seeking a divorce lawyer.

"You should get home and get a couple hours of sleep," Detective Allen advised him as he handed him a cup of coffee.

"I wish I could. I have a meeting with Parker today concerning the status of the Mason case. I think he wants to pass it off on somebody else so I can devote all of my time to the storage unit double homicide." Keys took a sip of his coffee. "And I haven't even had a chance to go through this yet."

Keys picked up Mac's cell phone and turned it on. Once it was on and unlocked, he began to go through it, not expecting to find anything. There was nothing in his call log, but when Keys got to his photo gallery, things got interesting.

Keys thought he was seeing things when he swiped by the first few images. "Hold the hell up," he said and went back to the beginning.

Detective Allen looked over at him, wondering what was going on. "What's going on? What is it?" He walked around the desk and stood behind Keys.

Keys held up the phone so Allen could see the pictures. "Who does that look like?" he asked Allen and watched his jaw drop slightly.

What he was looking at was a selfie of Mac and Spring. The two looked happy as they cheesed for the camera.

Keys swiped the phone again, going to the next picture of Spring and Mac hugged up in front of his car, and another with Spring kissing Mac's cheek. There were pictures as recent as a couple of weeks prior. As of about an hour ago, patrol units had informed him that Spring was at Trey's funeral. After further thought, he remembered the ballistics report indicating that there was DNA evidence of a woman on Mac, and also that Mac was the person who shot Trey in his home, but the person who had shot Mac was still unknown.

"So if Spring was Mac's girl, why would she be at Trey's funeral?" Keys asked. "We have to get this up to Parker. This is more than enough to get a warrant."

Fats picked up the kilo of heroin off the table and put it to his nose. He could smell the potency through the heavily wrapped square. The going rate on the streets for one brick of dope was anywhere from $60,000 to $70,000, depending on who you knew. Vick was letting it go for $45,000 a pop, which was the lowest in the hood.

"How much of this shit do you got?" Fats asked.

"Enough, but you better cop up 'cause I'm about to bag it up and hit the streets with it. You know once I do that it's going to be hard for any of you niggas to eat."

"Shit, well, let me get another one if that's the case. I got the money in my car."

Fats took Vick up on his offer. He didn't know how much of this stuff Vick had, but before the day was out, he was going to buy as much of it as his money could allow him to.

Burying Trey was one of the hardest things Spring had ever done in her life. As soon as Lou and a couple other people shoveled dirt over his casket, Spring finally began to cry. Reality set in fast that there was no way possible she would ever see him again, at least not in this world.

Spring left the cemetery feeling worse than when she was at the church. Despite everything that was weighing heavy on her heart, all she wanted to do was pop a Tylenol and forget about it all. She rode with Corey in silence, but every once in a while she could feel him glancing over at her, probably hoping that she would spark up a conversation, form a plan, something. But she was numb. She didn't want to think another thought.

"The police just got behind us," Corey said finally as he looked into the rearview mirror. "I didn't violate any traffic laws, so they shouldn't fuck with us."

All of the registration and insurance on the Range Rover was good, so Spring wasn't worried about that.

However, she did remove the pistol from her lap and put it in her bag. She'd changed into something more comfortable and she used the sneaker on her foot to kick the bag under the seat. Seconds later, the red and blue lights began to flash behind them.

"The registration and insurance are in the sun visor," Spring told Corey as he pulled over.

They sat there for a second before yet another cop car pulled up. Emerging from it were Detectives Keys and Allen with their guns drawn. As a precaution due to not knowing whether Spring was armed, they walked slowly toward the Range Rover, each on an opposite side of the vehicle. Keys tapped on the passenger side window where Spring sat.

"Spring, we're gonna need you to step out of the car," Keys said when she rolled the window down.

Spring looked at him like he was crazy.

"What do they need you to step out of the car for?" Corey asked in a low tone for only Spring's ears to hear. "Do you want me to pull off?"

Spring shook her head.

"There's a warrant for your arrest," Keys told her. "We have orders to take you in."

There was also a warrant to search her personal belongings and her immediate surroundings, but he wasn't going to tell her that until she got out of the car.

As soon as Spring opened her door and placed one foot on the ground she was arrested. Allen reached in and took the keys out of the ignition so Corey wouldn't be tempted to pull off. He too was taken out of the car and placed in handcuffs as a precaution. During the search, Allen found two guns, one in Spring's bag under the passenger's seat and the other one under the driver's seat. Spring tried to take ownership of that gun too, and for a second Detective Keys was going to let her, since it was her car.

Corey wasn't trying to hear it. He knew what Spring was thinking, but he'd never be able to live with himself if she took his beef too. Spring felt like there wasn't a reason for both of them to go to jail, and she didn't care about bruising his ego. If Corey could, he'd take ownership of the gun in her bag, just to lighten the burden on her. In fact, he had plans to do just that when he got down to the police station.

After selling Fats a couple of bricks, Vick had twenty-two left. Vick wasn't a drug dealer anymore so the product wasn't going as fast as he wanted it to go. The money he did have he was blowing it left and right just because it seemed unlimited. But in the eyes of anyone else, it was a fact that Vick was going to be broke.

Chapter 10

"I don't have anything to say to you until I see my lawyer," Spring repeated herself for the third time.

It seemed that Detective Keys wasn't getting it through his head. He was so desperate for answers he couldn't see through the smoke screen Spring was putting up. "Okay, fine. You don't have to say anything, but I want you to listen to me real clearly. You're in a whole lot of trouble, Ms. Stewart. Your fingerprints were at the scene of Mac's murder, and you coincidently know both Trey and Mac very well. I'm also sure that once we get this warrant for your DNA, it's going to come back that you were the one who had sex with him just hours before he was killed."

Spring sat there listening but looked off into space as if she wasn't at all entertained by what he was saying. Deep down she was shook, and the flickering light above the table she was sitting at wasn't making her feel any better. She had just wanted to get money and live well. She didn't know when everything had gone downhill.

"Now, I know you weren't the one who killed Trey, but I can bet any amount of money that you killed Mac." Detective Keys was sure of it. After piecing together what evidence he had on her thus far, she became the prime suspect.

The door opened and Allen strolled into the room with a grin on his face. He slammed a thin folder onto the table in front of Keys. "These are the surveillance photos from the ATM machine across the street from the auto body shop. And guess who could be seen going in and coming out a couple of days ago."

Detective Keys turned a couple of pictures around so Spring could see them. "That looks just like you. And again, I bet the house on the notion that you went in there to pawn Mac's jewelry," Keys said. "Hell, I might be going out on a limb, but I think you might've even had something to do with Mike's death."

Spring was on the verge of panic, but she didn't show any concern. She just sat there, not saying a word, but rather taking a mental note of all the evidence. Keys had pretty much hit everything on the nose, except for what happened to Mike. He was right; Spring was in a lot of trouble and she was going to have to come up with something remarkable to get out of it.

This time, the judge denied bail, pending her next court appearance, which was a month away. She was sick that she had to be taken to the county jail. On the bus ride there, other prisoners described the place as nothing less than a hell hole. They were not lying either. From the moment she got into R&D, her stomach turned from the foul smell in the air.

"Don't worry about it, girl. It's not that bad once you get up to the pod," a female in the seat next to Spring said. "My name is Jewels."

"Look, sweetheart, I don't mean to sound rude, but I'm not trying to make any new friends," Spring spoke lightly.

The female respected it, understanding exactly how Spring was feeling about being in jail. She wasn't mad at her in the least. So instead of pushing her limits she sat in silence.

The rest of the intake process was irritating for Spring. She was fingerprinted, her picture was taken, and she was asked a series of questions. The worst part was when she had to be strip searched by a female guard who made her do all kinds of embarrassing things. Feeling another woman's finger up her anus digging around her insides looking for God knows what made her feel low. It wasn't over fast enough. She was then dressed in county blues and given a bedroll, only to be kicked back into the holding cell. She had to wait for a correctional officer to take her and a bunch of other girls upstairs to the pod.

The first thing Corey did when he went home was take a nice hot shower. The water ran down his face and onto his chest as he let his thoughts run wild. His original plans to tell the cops the guns were his went out the window when they released him at the scene. The detective was so focused on taking in Spring that he told the cops to release Corey without even asking him for identification. As soon as he walked through the door, he called down to the courthouse and heard all about the bad news with Spring. There was nothing that he could do for her but keep her lawyer paid up and keep money on her books. He'd done a bid himself, and it was almost like he was living vicariously through Spring. The whole process seemed to have started over again.

He got out of the shower and went to dry off and put some clothes on. While he was in his room getting dressed, a semihard knock on his door got his attention. He wasn't expecting anyone, and since he had drama on the streets and it was at an all-time high, Corey wasn't trying to get caught slipping. He grabbed the 10 mm off his dresser then slowly crept to the front door. The knocks continued and got harder.

"Yo, who the fuck is it?" Corey yelled with his gun pointed at the door.

"It's Lou, nigga, and lower that mafuckin' gun," Lou said from the other side the door.

Corey was still cautious in opening the door, and it wasn't until he saw Lou's face that he relaxed a little. "How did you know I had a gun pointed at the door?" Corey asked. He stepped to the side so Lou could enter.

Lou smiled. "'Cause I know you. We all got some of my father's habits."

Corey couldn't deny that. "So, what's goin' on? Are you good?"

"Nah, I heard you and Spring got booked the other day after my dad's funeral. Is she cool?" Lou flopped on the couch. Lou smiled at the serious look on Corey's face. Corey was shocked that Lou knew about it because he surely didn't tell anyone. "Come on, man. I got my ways," Lou said.

"Yeah, you're just like ya pops. But anyway, Spring is still in the can. I talked to her lawyer this morning and he said he was all over it. He said he was going to petition the court to reconsider its ruling."

"Damn, that's fucked up. So what do you wanna do about Vick? I heard about that crutty mufucka too," Lou based.

"Damn, li'l nigga, you do know a lot. Hell, do you know where I can find that nigga at?"

"Shit, if you want me to, I can find him before the day is out. But I'll only do it if I can be with you when you go and put that work in. When he became disloyal to the crew, he became disloyal to my pops. I take that shit personal."

Corey couldn't believe the way that Lou was talking, but then again, he was the son of a street genius. A man who carried strong morals and lived on family values. In fact, after he thought about it, Corey kind of expected Lou to step up to the plate one day. Corey took Lou up on his offer just to see if he was ready. Said it was a one-shot thing, so he hoped that he held true to his word and found Vick like he said he would.

Benny sat poolside with his feet in the water, watching his daughter swim back and forth. She, along with several other kids, had taken advantage of the new indoor recreational swimming pool grand opening.

"Swim, Kayla, swim!" Benny yelled.

Santana walked in and squatted down next to Benny. He spoke in a low tone. "Let me know what the word is. I got my boys ready to move out right now," Santana said.

Since the funeral, Benny hadn't heard anything and, as patient as he tried to be, it was running short. It didn't look like he was going to get his dope or his money. That posed a real problem. The last thing he wanted to do was appear to be weak within his own organization. The penalties had to be swift and brutal, just to make a statement.

"Kill them, and that includes Vick. Make sure you get it done quietly. I don't want the hood spreading rumors that we were beefing with them. We don't need the law snooping around my business," Benny said before turning his attention back to his daughter in the water.

It was official. Benny had given the green light on the hit, and Santana was more than willing to carry it out.

Corey drove toward the south side while Lou sat on the passenger side, tracking Vick down on his phone.

Because of Trey, Lou was well connected to the hood and had key players in every section of the city that he could call on if necessary. Needless to say, eight strong phone calls later, he had a pinpoint location on Vick.

"The nigga been movin' work out of the Tropical Inn. It's a rinky-dink motel right in the back of Center City," Lou informed him. "Room 106, and he's pushing an all-white Aztec rental car."

Corey looked over at him and was impressed with the intel he had gotten on such a short notice. Now it was time to see if any of it would pan out. It took Corey every bit of twenty minutes to get downtown, and when they finally got to the motel, the white Aztec rental was sitting in the parking lot among several other cars.

"Damn, that's the car right there," Lou pointed out.

Instead of parking in the Tropical Inn lot, Corey pulled in across the street to another motel's parking lot.

"Stay here. I'll be right back," Corey said and pulled the 10 mm out from under his seat.

"You shittin' me. You already know my intentions," Lou replied. He pulled out his own weapon, a compact .45, from his waist and cocked a bullet into the chamber.

Corey didn't even know he had a gun.

"We doing this shit together," Lou said as he got out of the car. There was no point in arguing with him, so Corey didn't; he just got out of the car too.

"Just be careful, little nigga," he told Lou as they headed for the motel. "I don't have time for some shit to happen to you too."

Corey felt the hood of the Aztec to see if it was still hot. It was warm, meaning Vick must have just returned from somewhere. When they got up to room 106, Corey put his ear to the door while Lou looked through a small crack in the blinds. The sound of the TV was the only thing they heard.

"Watch out," Corey said and reared back to kick in the door.

With one kick and a loud thud, the door flew open. The duffle bag of dope was in plain sight on the bed. Just before they entered the room, Lou saw Vick come around the corner outside with a McDonald's bag in one hand and a burger in the other. Lou raised his gun, and when he locked eyes with Vick, Lou let them fly.

Vick dropped his bag and burger, and instead of fleeing, he dipped behind one of the parked cars and drew his own weapon. Corey cut his eyes at Lou, silently cursing him for not giving a warning, but then he too turned his attention on Vick. They exchanged bullets like they were in the Old West. Vick could see that he was outnumbered, and he didn't have that many rounds left in his clip to win a battle against them.

"Shit," Vick said to himself, looking around for an escape.

The gunfire had subsided for a second and Vick knew that Corey was either walking him down or they were reloading. Either way, he wasn't trying to stick around to find out. He jumped up from behind the car and started shooting again.

Corey and Lou got low behind the car, which gave Vick the opportunity to run.

"Get the dope!" Corey told Lou and then took off behind Vick.

Bullets whizzed by Vick's head, and he was grateful when they found homes in the cars parked around him versus in his skull. It also made him run faster. Cop sirens could be heard in the distance.

The more distance Vick put between him and Corey, the more Corey realized that he wasn't going to catch him. He was also almost out of bullets.

"Fuck!" Corey yelled out. He ended the chase and slowed to a jog.

Corey ducked behind some trash cans when two of the many cop cars out there drove by him. Not wanting to risk being seen, he crawled behind some high bushes on the side of someone's house. Corey pulled out his phone and attempted to call Lou so he could hurry up and come get him. He was sure somebody had reported all of the gunfire, and he wanted to clear the area, and fast.

"The DNA test came back positive," Detective Allen said. He set the folder on Keys's desk. "She's our girl."

Keys sat back in his chair and began to look at the papers. It was amazing to him that just days prior they didn't have any evidence to work with, and then, poof! Just like that, they had their prime suspect in the homicide cases.

"All right, we have her DNA on one of the victims, her prints at the scene of the crime, and she's still not saying anything. Did we get the ballistics back on the two guns she was locked up with?" Keys asked.

Unfortunately, the ballistics on neither of the guns were a match to the shell casings found in Mac's room. No fingerprints were on the shell casings, either. The task of putting Spring at the scene of the crime during the time it was being committed was an uphill battle.

In the court of law, all Detective Keys had was circumstantial evidence. It was strong circumstantial evidence, but it was by no means a slam dunk case, especially since Spring's lawyer specialized in jury trial. Out of the eighteen homicide cases he had taken to trial, McMan had only lost one, and in that case the defendant was pointed out by well over six witnesses who saw him pull the trigger. The evidence in their case was much less than that. No witnesses, no smoking gun, and some circumstantial evidence that could be refuted with the right statement. Detective Keys needed a little more if he really wanted to win.

Chapter 11

Spring walked out into the visiting room thinking that she was about to get a legal visit. To her surprise, it was Summer, who began to cry immediately after seeing her sister in a prison uniform.

"Come on, girl, don't be all up in here crying," Spring said and gave Summer a hug. "Somebody might think I'm soft and try to take my cookies," she joked, making Summer laugh a little. "Now how in the world did you know that I was locked up?"

Spring hadn't called and told anybody yet about her being in jail, so seeing her sister standing in front of her was a total shock. The two women sat down before Summer began to talk.

"I don't know. I . . . I just felt that something was wrong with you. Mama said she hadn't heard from you in a few days, and you weren't answering your phone. Something told me to check here. I went online and checked all the hospitals and jails and there you were. In the county jail on a gun charge. A gun charge!" Summer stared into Spring's eyes. "What the hell is going on with you, Spring? I knew it had to be something. With the house and all that money, but jail?"

Spring avoided Summer's stare.

"Spring, look at me," Summer snapped. "Talk to me. And don't lie."

Spring couldn't lie to her even if she wanted to. "I got into some trouble," Spring began. "But everything is going to be all right. I just gotta get out of here."

At that moment, reality set in. She'd kept telling herself that everything would be okay, but she knew deep down that it wouldn't. Between the murders and the missing product, she was in dire straits. The feds were trying to hem her up, and if they didn't have their way with her, then Benny would definitely step in. He wasn't playing about his drugs, and he had no problem giving people dirt naps. While Spring was sitting inside the jail all safe and sound, she knew everyone she loved was in danger.

"Spring, let me help you. I wanna help you!"

"No, no, no. My lawyer said that he was going to make something—"

"Fuck that lawyer, Spring. I'm sitting right here and now!" Summer spoke in a quick, hushed tone. "Whatever you need me to do I'll do it. If it will get you out of here, I'll do it."

"I'm not gonna put ya life at risk for some shit that I did to myself," Spring said with tears in her eyes. "I can't."

"Spring . . . Spring, remember when we were younger? We always had each other's back no matter what. There's nothing out there in those streets that I can't handle. Please, sis, just let me help you. If you can't depend on me to be there for you, how can you call me your sister? Who else you got?"

At that point, the tears were running freely down Spring's face. She really didn't want anything to happen to Summer. At the same time, if she just sat there and did nothing, Summer's life was going to be at risk anyway.

"I swear, if I let you help me, you gotta do exactly what I tell you to do when I tell you to do it. And as soon as I get out of here, I'm pulling you out."

"You have my word."

Spring wiped the tears from her face, took in a deep breath, and began to give Summer the rundown on what was really going on.

***

Corey and Lou sat in Corey's house at the dining room table, counting the money that they took from Vick. It looked like a lot, but there was only around twenty-five grand with him, and it was in denominations of fives and tens.

"Yo, you slow as hell. You let that nigga outrun you." Lou laughed as he reached over and passed Corey a blunt. "I don't think you should be smoking on this." He chuckled some more.

"Man, my knee fucked up and I been shot twice," Corey offered up his excuses. "And you damn sure left me in those bushes long enough. It was starting to get cold out in those bitches. Good thing I had my hoodie on."

"Shit, if I would have come and got you any sooner, we'd both be in jail right now. The cops were everywhere."

Despite Corey having to stay in the bushes for four hours, coupled with the fact that Vick got away, they were able to recover around twelve bricks of Benny's dope and the twenty-five grand. Money-wise, they were still short about a half million, and as far as the dope, they were short thirteen bricks. Benny wasn't going to accept half of his product. With him, it was all or nothing.

"Damn, we really gotta find this nigga," Corey said. He took a toke of the blunt. "You think you can work ya magic again? 'Cause you was quick with the info last time."

Lou shrugged. He wasn't sure if he could. Vick was running scared, so nine times out of ten he was going to be laying as low as possible. Corey read the doubt on his face and nodded. There were only a couple of things that could make him come out from hiding, and before Corey rested his head tonight, he was going to explore all of the angles. He wanted Vick dead in the worst way, and even if he did it with his last breath, Corey was going to kill

Vick, or at least be there when the angel of death bucked his number.

The one-hour visit was hardly enough time to give Summer all of the game. She'd barely scratched the surface of what she did for a living. But, still, Spring managed to tell her the most important things that Summer needed to know. It was a lot for Summer to take in, but she got the gist of it.

"A'ight, come back up here tomorrow," Spring said then got up and hugged Summer in farewell.

"I got you, sis," Summer said before she walked away.

Everything inside of Spring said that bringing Summer into her world was a bad idea, and there were a few times during the visit that she wanted to tell her to forget about it. The only thing that kept her from doing so was the fact that Summer had her mind made up that she was going to do something to help. Since that was the case, Spring wanted to make sure that her sister was fully equipped.

The streets could get ugly in a New York minute. If something were to happen to Summer out there, the only thing that would be able to save the city from Spring's wrath was God Himself. People wouldn't even want to come outside. Street corners would look like ghost towns, and nobody would eat until Benny and everyone he dealt with was six feet under the ground. For everybody's sake, she hoped that it all worked out.

Fats was sitting in his car with one of his hood rats leaning over from the passenger seat giving him head. He grabbed his phone off the dashboard, aimed it down, and took a picture of the female going to work.

"You better not post that shit," the female took his dick out of her mouth and said.

Fats grabbed her by the back of her head and pushed his dick back inside her mouth. Right when he was about to do the opposite of what she had just asked him, the phone began to ring.

"Yo, what up, playboy," Fats answered, seeing that it was Vick calling.

Corey had taken all of his money, so Vick was trying to get rid of the rest of the dope. "Yo, the prices went down."

"Whoa, whoa, you gotta watch how you talk on these phones. If the feds are listening, we don't want them to get the wrong idea," Fats said. "Yeah, but I heard you had a 2015 Yukon Denali for sale. How much do you want for it?" Fats corrected him with his code talk.

Vick caught right on. "You know they want like fifty thousand if you get it off the lot. But being that my car is used, I'll give it to you for thirty-five. Oh, and I got a nice gray 2011 Tahoe for ya wife. If you get it right now, I'll give it to you for thirty."

Fats sat there in silence thinking about the conversation he and Chill had the other night. The word was on the streets that he had robbed Corey for the work. And since Corey had been looking for him day in and day out, Fats thought that it had to be for the dope.

Buying another brick after knowing what he knew just wouldn't be right. The shit needed to stop.

"Yo, let me holla at my wife and I'll call you right back." Fats hung up the phone.

He was cool with Vick, but he had love for Corey. Before, he wasn't going to get involved in it, but now he had made a choice and picked a side. He knew that once he made the call, Vick was good as dead. Fats briefly looked down at the girl giving him head, then looked back at his phone. Scrolling through his phone, he got to Corey's number and said, "Fuck it."

Summer stood in Spring's bedroom looking at herself in the vanity mirror on top of the dresser. She didn't have to do too much of anything to look like her sister. Her attitude was the only thing that needed to be adjusted. She had to go from being the nice, soft, and gentle person that she was to a bad girl. She had to think like Spring, react to certain situations like Spring and, most importantly, Summer had to become violent like Spring. That was going to be the biggest challenge for her. The street code that Spring had adopted was something else.

"You can do it," Summer told her reflection.

She tried to act tough.

"What? Don't make me shoot you. I will," she threatened and pointed her finger at the mirror as if it were a gun.

She had to laugh at her own words, hearing how proper she sounded.

Summer knew a little bit of the street slang and could even be a little sassy, but it was nothing like her sister. Summer was going to have to work on it fast if she had any chance of convincing people that she was Spring.

Summer's thoughts were interrupted by the sound of a door opening and closing downstairs. She knew for sure that it wasn't Spring, whom she'd just left at the jail, and according to Spring no one knew where she lived.

Summer walked over and grabbed a P.80 Ruger off the bed, stood by the bedroom door, and listened for the footsteps. There were none, so Summer made her way to the hallway and down the steps. She kept the gun down by her side the whole time, and when she finally made it downstairs, she heard noises coming from the kitchen.

Cupping both hands around the gun, she cautiously walked to the kitchen. When she got to the door and saw that it was her mom, Summer quickly tucked the gun into her back waistline before Ms. Gloria turned around.

"Aaaaaahhhhhhhhh!" Ms. Gloria screamed. She cocked back the knife in her hand when Summer came in out of nowhere.

Summer jumped back with her hands up. "Whoa, Mom! It's me!"

Ms. Gloria looked at Summer and quickly identified her. "Summer, you scared the shit out of me! Why aren't you in school?" She held her hand to her chest, trying to catch her breath.

Summer walked over and gave her mother a hug for scaring her. "I'm sorry, Mom. I had a break, so I decided to come and check up on Spring," she lied and avoided eye contact.

Ms. Gloria knew that she was lying, and after looking deeper into her eyes, she challenged Summer. "Now you know lying is a sin. Why are you really here, and where's that crazy-ass sister of yours? I been trying to call her for days."

Summer couldn't lie for a second time, and though she didn't want to give her mother the bad news about Spring's situation, she had to. She only told her that Spring was locked up, but that was more than enough to break her heart. Telling her the rest of the story wasn't an option, nor was it necessary at that point.

"Look, Mom, I have to go and take care of a few things. I'll take you up to the jail with me tomorrow," Summer told her. Seeing the crushed look on her mother's face, she touched her arm tenderly. "It's not as bad as it seems, so try not to worry."

She didn't have that much time to sit and talk, so she exited quickly before she was forced to watch her mother cry. It was time for her to get the show on the road.

Corey sat in his car, waiting for Fats to hit him back with the whole scoop on Vick. He still had dope left over, so Corey wanted to try to get more of it back before he killed Vick.

"A'ight, so look, I'll call you back later to set up a time and a place for us to meet up," Lou said into his cell phone. When he hung up, Corey looked over at him.

"Who was that?" Corey asked since Lou had been on the phone for fifteen minutes. He wasn't ear hustling on purpose, but he'd heard Lou say something about Trey.

"Aww, that was just a friend of my pops. Good dude," Lou responded.

Corey was about to inquire further about the guy, but his phone rang. His heart pounded when he saw Spring's face pop up on his screen. "Yo, what up?"

"Hey, I need you to come get me. I'm standing outside of the county jail."

Corey was already en route before she could get her next words out. He drove his way through all the traffic and took some back roads to cut through certain areas. It took him only ten minutes to get there when it should have taken him thirty minutes. He pulled right up in front of the jail, got out, and walked up to who he thought was Spring.

"You good?" He gave her a hug and a kiss on the cheek.

"Yeah, I'm good. I'm hungry as shit, though."

Lou got out of the car and gave her a hug too. Summer had no idea who he was, but she didn't make it known. She figured he must have been somebody Spring knew, so she hugged him back. As they were getting into the car, the phone call that Corey was waiting for finally came through. Fats explained the whole situation in code, giving a time and a location where Vick was supposed to meet up with him.

"Yo, homie, I really appreciate you on this one," Corey said and ended the phone call.

"So, what's the move?" he asked.

Summer sat there thinking about all the things Spring had told her thus far. "Let's try to see if we can get the stuff back first. I definitely need to get Benny's shit back. If he don't have it, then you already know what to do."

Corey was a few steps ahead of her and couldn't wait to put a bullet in Vick's head. For being disloyal, robbing them of their money, and trying to kill them, death was what Vick deserved.

Spring hadn't been out of her cell all night and hadn't eaten breakfast, lunch, or dinner. The only thing she was able to eat was the fruit that came with just about every meal. Words couldn't explain how stressed out she was with leaving her sister, mother, and her few friends out there in harm's way. She felt helpless and wanted to be out there so bad.

"Damn, celly, you been in here all day," Karan, Spring's cell buddy, said when she walked into the room. "It's about to be lockdown and we got a 'one shower a day' rule up in here."

Spring smiled for the first time in days. "I'm about to get in."

"Well, you better hurry up 'cause Fat Muffin is about to get in too. She's always trying to hit on somebody and, trust me, ya cute ass is her type." Karan laughed while drying her hair.

"Can I ask you something?" Spring said as she looked out the narrow window, watching the cars driving back and forth on the highway, which was visible from the jail. "What did you do to end up in a place like this?"

Every cell mate had asked Karan that question. The answer always remained the same. "My boyfriend liked to put his hands on me. He used to do awful things to me. Sometimes, I wouldn't even recognize my face after he was done with me. It got to the point where it was him or me, and let's just say that he won't be able to punch me anymore."

"Damn, you down for a homicide?" Spring asked.

"Nah, I didn't kill the nigga. I wish I would have. But one night I cooked a bangin'-ass dinner, and while he was sitting at the dinner table, I took a meat cleaver and cut his hand off."

Visions of slamming the cleaver down on her boy-friend's wrist and severing it completely flashed through Karan's mind. Spring was surprised, but if she were in Karan's shoes she would have done the exact same thing, if not worse. Spring hated abusive men, and she wished a man would ever try her like that.

"Look, we can chop it up about all that shit when you get out the shower, though," Karan told her.

Spring, who didn't feel like dealing with Fat Muffin, agreed and grabbed her bag then headed for the shower. Karan was the only person who seemed to be cool, and Spring couldn't wait to come back and converse about the streets.

Vick sat in his car and watched as Fats pulled up and parked a few cars down. The night sky made a perfect cover for Corey, who walked down the street from the opposite direction unseen. Even when Vick got out of his car and looked around, he still didn't notice Corey.

"Damn, playboy, what it look like," Fats greeted him when he got out of his car with a small book bag in his hand. "You keep playing and I'ma end up buying every-thing you got, my nigga." He passed Vick the bag.

"Shit, nigga, I wish you would hurry up," Vick shot back as he opened the bag to check the money.

The whole time he had his head down, Corey was creeping up on him from behind with his gun pointed at his head. Fats took a step back, not wanting to get brain matter all over him. His move prompted Vick to lift his head up, and when he did, the barrel of Corey's gun pressed against the back of his head. The only thing Vick was waiting for was the blast.

"Damn, Fats, you set me up?" Vick asked with his face twisted. "You bitch-made-ass nigga."

Before Vick could get another word out, a black Cadillac CTS pulled up right beside them. First, Vick was searched and then stripped of his weapon; then he was cracked upside the back of his head and thrown into the back seat.

"Good lookin' out, homie," Corey said and passed Fats the bag of money back.

"Anytime, my nigga. Anytime. I don't like that snake shit. Handle your business," Fats said.

Detective Keys, Detective Allen, Head Detective Parker, and District Attorney Nicole Madeline all sat in her office discussing the next step in the case. In most homicide cases, there was some form of evidence that made the case stronger. A gun, eyewitnesses, DNA evidence, ballistic evidence and, in some cases, a confession by the suspect. The DA didn't have any of those things in this case.

However, there was more than enough circumstantial evidence to put Spring at the scene of the crime. She could also be the reason Mac's jewelry ended up at Mike's auto body shop. Evidence indicated that she knew both of the victims, and footage from her social media pages of her firing a gun at the shooting range could prove that she was familiar with how to use a gun. Not only that, but there was also reason to believe that Spring had something to do with the double homicide at the storage facility. Even with all the information presented to her, the DA still didn't believe that she had enough. It was probably enough for her to bring formal charges, but not enough evidence to prove Spring's guilt at trial. There was one other thing that would strengthen this case, and DA Madeline wanted the cherry on top.

"Go and get a confession," Madeline told everybody before ending the meeting. "We need that confession if we are going to take this case anywhere."

Chapter 12

While Spring was walking back from the chow hall at breakfast time, her name was called out over the intercom, telling her to report to the visiting room.

Something is wrong, she thought as she walked down the long corridor.

When she got to the visiting room, she expected to see Summer, but then the guard pointed to the legal cubicle. Her lawyer, along with Detectives Keys and Allen, were sitting there waiting for her.

"Wassup, McMan?" she greeted him when she entered the room.

McMan nodded at the detective for them to give him and Spring a moment alone. Only when the door was closed did McMan speak.

"I know, I know. Before you say anything, trust me, I know what you're thinking. They called me early this morning, saying that they were going to charge you with a double homicide if you didn't give a statement."

"A double homicide?" Spring asked incredulously.

"Yes, but all they have is a bunch of circumstantial evidence. Now I'm going to ask you a few questions, so be as honest with me as you can."

McMan didn't want to know if she had committed the crime. To him, it didn't matter if she did or didn't. What he did want were answers pertaining to the circumstantial evidence the DA was going to base her case off. He wanted to make sure that as the conversation progressed, Spring's answers didn't incriminate her. After a few minutes of conversation, McMan felt like she was ready to talk to the detectives.

"Keep your answers short and sweet," McMan advised Spring before standing up and waving the detectives into the room.

"Okay, Spring, we have a lot to go over. So let's just get right to it," Keys said. He took a seat and unzipped his briefcase. "So what is your relationship to Trey and Mac?"

"Well, I was dating both of them at one point, and even at the same time. I broke up with Mac about two months ago, but we were still sexually active. That's why I was at his house."

"And what time did you leave Mac's house?" Allen cut in.

"It had to be around three-thirty or close to four. I try not to spend the night when we have sex. I don't want any old feelings to come creeping back in."

Keys and Allen went hard with the interview, trying to catch Spring in a lie, but she stood firm and kept it simple, not going in too deep, but giving them just enough. She denied taking any of Mac's jewelry, and when asked about her trip to Mike's auto body shop, she said that Mac had pawned some of her earrings among some of his other pieces of jewelry. She said that she was down there trying to buy the jewelry back. Spring told them that Mike wanted too much money for the earrings.

All of her stories were backed up by the evidence that had been collected thus far. They knew that she was lying about something, but they couldn't pinpoint what it was. The story would sound believable to the average person, so Keys decided to leave that situation alone.

Spring thought that she was done and had put on a great performance, but Detective Keys wasn't done. Now it was time to get into the incident that happened with the Washington Avenue shooting, along with the Orange Storage Company homicides. He wasn't about to take it easy on her. She didn't know it, but she wasn't out of the hot seat just yet.

Vick sat in the middle of the room with his hands tied behind his back. Summer sat on the arm of the couch, watching while Lou sized him up with a baseball bat in his hands.

"Damn, li'l man, ya pops would be proud of you right now." Vick chuckled, looking up at Lou.

That smart remark earned him a vicious blow to the kneecap. Vick felt the blow through his whole body, and when he opened his mouth to scream in agony, Lou muffled it by stuffing a washcloth damn near down his throat.

Summer waited until the pain subsided before she spoke to Vick. "Why don't you just give me the dope?" Summer got off the couch and walked over to him. "This shit is only about to get ugly for you."

She pulled the rag out of his mouth so he could talk. His breathing was heavy, but he still managed to talk through his deep breaths. "You must think I'm a fuckin' fool. As soon as I give you the dope, you gon' kill me anyway. As long as I got the dope, yo' ass is in just as much trouble that I'm in right now. Benny is gonna kill all of y'all." He chuckled. "So, fuck you."

Summer stuck the rag back into his mouth, then stepped back. Lou took the bat and cracked him in his other knee. The pain hurt so bad that time, Vick almost flipped out of the chair.

"I don't think he's gonna tell us where the dope is," Corey said to Summer. "He knows he's about to die, so there's no need for him to help us out."

"Yeah, I think he's right," Lou chimed in. "Let's just kill his bitch ass and get it over with."

Summer walked back over and took a seat on the arm of the couch. Her thoughts went into overdrive. *Think, Summer, think,* she said to herself. *What in the hell would Spring do?*

It took Summer a few minutes to process her thoughts, but then a good idea came to her. "How many bricks of dope do we have right now?" she asked Corey.

He reached over and grabbed the bag sitting next to the couch and threw it onto the coffee table. "There are twelve bricks in here, and we still don't know what this stupid mafucka did with the money. Why, what are you thinking about?" he asked.

She would be going out on a limb with her idea, but it seemed like something Spring would do in the situation. Just killing Vick wasn't going to make anything better, so instead of doing so, Summer was going to use his worthless life as much as she was able.

"Fuck him up some more then put his ass in the car. We're about to take a ride," Summer said then walked off to the bathroom so she wouldn't have to see the beat down that she'd just ordered. Lou went straight to work and knocked Vick's front teeth clear down his throat with the baseball bat.

Spring got back to her cell and jumped right up in her bed, not saying a word to Karan, who was sitting at the table reading the Bible. She had a lot of shit on her mind and was stressed out to the max. The rest of the interview with the detectives didn't go too well. Though she kept her answers short and sweet, they didn't really make that much sense. She started fumbling with her words concerning the shootout on Washington Avenue with Vick and the cops and the double homicide that happened at the storage company. It got so crazy in there, McMan had to end the interview.

"Whatever you got going on wit' you, always remember that there's no burden in this world that God can't lift off of you," Karan looked up and told Spring. "All you gotta do is ask Him to get you out of any difficulty you may be experiencing."

With all due respect, Spring wasn't trying to hear anything about God or Karan's preaching. Stuff had just gotten real, and now the detectives were trying their best to put one of the murders on her. She could tell by their line of questioning that they were trying to brew up something nice for her. In any case, she was facing the death penalty or, at the bare minimum, a life sentence in a women's prison. The detectives had made that clear. Spring wasn't about that jail life.

Benny ended his phone call with Luv and then walked to the front of the restaurant. Santana and a few of his boys were there. He didn't have enough dope to last him through the week, so it was a must that he put another order in.

"A'ight, I got a pickup for tomorrow. I want you and Jesus to make the run," Benny told Santana. "Did you take care of the other thing?" Benny asked.

As Santana was answering the question, the bells on top of the front door began to chime, causing everybody to look up. Santana and Jesus jumped up from their seats when Summer dragged Vick through the door by his collar. They drew their guns when they saw that she had a gun in her hand.

"Whoa, whoa!" Benny yelled, stopping Santana and Jesus from firing their weapons. He noticed that Corey had a duffle bag over his shoulder as well.

Summer got to the middle of the restaurant and dropped Vick to the ground. He was beaten up pretty bad, but he was still alive.

"Speak of the devil," Benny said and walked over to her. "You know, we were just about to come kill you and your friends."

Summer looked at Benny then over his shoulder at Jesus and Santana, who still had their guns aimed at her. "Not quite," she said. She took the duffle bag from Corey's shoulder and set it on the floor. "It's twelve bricks in there, and this guy act like he don't want to tell me where the rest of it is." Summer smacked Vick on the side of his head with her gun.

Benny wasn't happy at all with the news. "So, you kill my people, take my dope, and now you come into my establishment—"

"First off, I didn't kill ya people," Summer cut him off. "It was this piece of shit who killed ya people."

"Nah, Benny, she's lying. Shoot that bitch," Vick yelled out from the floor in his final attempt to get out of the situation.

Summer reached into her back pocket and pulled out a copy of Spring's police report. "How could I kill anybody when I was locked up that night?" Summer passed Benny the paperwork. "He had Mike killed, stole the dope, and tried to kill me. He tried to make it look like I was the one who did it."

Benny read the police report, checking the times and the dates on the arrest. It all checked out, which meant that Vick was lying to him.

"Okay, let's just say that this piece of shit did do everything that you said he did. What, are you not still responsible for the members of your crew? You expect me to just take the loss and forget about it?" Benny quizzed her with an unenthused look on his face.

"Nah, I'm not asking you to chalk it up. I'm just asking you for a chance to make it right. I need some more time to come up with the rest of the money. I'm giving you half ya dope back, the man who killed ya brother, and my word that I will come up with five hundred thousand dollars. I will add an extra two hundred grand to it as a sign of gratitude for your patience," Summer explained. She looked into Benny's eyes with sincerity.

"So when will I have my money?" Benny asked. "And don't say anything crazy."

"To be honest with you, I can't give you an exact date. This piece of shit took some money from me as well. So I'm pretty much starting from scratch," Summer expressed.

Though Benny was hot under the collar, he did respect this bold move from Spring. It was the way she came; but at the end of the day, Benny wanted his money.

"You got two weeks," Benny said and held up two fingers. "I need my money in two weeks and not a day later. You can leave now."

Summer didn't move and neither did Corey. Her business wasn't concluded yet. She knew Corey wasn't trying to leave until he knew that Vick was dead.

"We can't leave until he's dead," Summer said then pointed her gun at Vick.

She was hoping that Benny took the lead in the killing because she'd never shot anybody before, let alone taken a life. Summer was scared to death.

"Look, I know you want him dead and, believe me, he's going to die, but this muthafucka killed my brother and I'm not just gonna put a bullet in his head. That would be too easy. Me and my boys are going to have a little fun with him, if you don't mind."

"He has to die," Corey cut in.

"And, trust me, he will. I give you my word on that."

Corey wasn't too convinced.

"How about if he's not dead by the end of the night, you can keep whatever you owe me?" Benny offered.

Corey and Summer looked at each other. Summer had the gun pointed at Vick's head. Her hands were sweating, her heart was racing, and all eyes were on her. She was afraid they would realize how nervous she was and her cover would be blown, but she was more anxious at the thought of having to take a man's life. When she agreed to help her sister, she knew she was walking into dangerous territory, and she knew she was going to have to do some crazy things, but murder was not one of them. She glanced over at Corey, silently praying that he would agree to Benny's offer.

"Let him deal with it," Corey said. He nodded for Summer to leave with him.

Vick had killed Benny's brother, and now Benny knew it for sure, so there was no way possible Vick was going to get up and leave. Vick was going to die, and probably in the worst way.

"We'll be back in two weeks," Summer told Benny then turned around and headed for the front door.

Benny could see that Spring was about her business and, for that, he had a newfound respect for her. Of course, he wasn't about to tell her that, but it was there. He also felt confident that she was going to come through with his money. The set of morals she displayed were ones that he was all too familiar with.

Chapter 13

"Mom, just calm down," Summer said as she and Ms. Gloria stood in the line to get into the visiting room. Ms. Gloria couldn't wait to give Spring a piece of her mind, and Summer was starting to regret telling her to meet at the jail so they could visit Spring together.

When they finally got into the visiting room, Summer pleaded one last time to her mother not to snap on Spring. Those pleas went into one ear and right out of the other because as soon as Spring came onto the visiting room floor, Ms. Gloria let her have it.

"Don't hug me. Sit yo' narrow ass down," she snapped. "You must like being in jail. What in the hell is wrong wit' you? I just bailed ya ass out the other day, and now you ridin' around with another gun on you?"

Spring cut her eyes over at Summer, wondering why in the hell she'd brought their mother up there.

"I told ya ass about ripping and running around in those streets like you crazy. You not gon' be happy until you give me a heart attack."

Ms. Gloria went from speaking out of anger to talking with her heart. Spring couldn't do anything but sit there and listen to her mother vent. Her mother's words of concern had her tearing up a little.

"All right, Mom, cut her some slack," Summer intervened, feeling bad for her sister.

The problem with that was Ms. Gloria turned her attention to her now. "Yo' ass better not even think about being out there in those streets. And why haven't yo' ass been back to school yet? Let me find out yo' ass is out here doing things ya behind ain't got no business doing. Yo' ass will be sitting right next to her in the same damn jumpsuit."

If Ms. Gloria didn't have a doctor's appointment in the next hour, she would have stayed there grinding the twins up. "Now get yo' ass up and give me a hug," Ms. Gloria said as she prepared to leave.

While she was hugging Spring, she whispered a few words to her: "I love you, baby. I just don't want nothing to happen to you. I don't want this type of life for you. Please, baby, come home and stay out of trouble." She kissed Spring up and down the side of her face.

Before Ms. Gloria left, she promised that she would be back up there sometime that weekend, something Spring wanted so she could sit down and talk to her mom.

"Damn, Summer, why did you have to tell her and then bring her up here?" Spring said when she sat back down.

"First of all, you know I wasn't going to be able to keep this from Mom for too long. Second of all, I didn't bring her. She insisted on coming to see you and drove herself here. But, girl, don't worry about Mama. She'll be a'ight," Summer said as she watched Ms. Gloria walk out the door.

That wasn't the point, but Spring didn't want to get into it right then. There were more serious things to discuss. "So, what's going on out there?" she asked.

"Girl, you live a crazy life," Summer replied, thinking about everything that had gone down. "We found Vick, and we got some of the dope back."

Summer was quiet for a second, thinking about the look on Vick's face when she left him with Benny. Spring could tell by the look in Summer's eyes that she wasn't the same. She knew that something had happened, and it was more than likely Vick's murder.

"Who did it, Corey?"

"No, it was Benny. I'm glad I didn't have to do it. I don't know if I would have been able to."

"Are you okay?"

"Yeah, I'm good. You did say that he was trying to kill you, right?"

"Yes, and I'm sorry that you had to go through that. I told you these streets is crazy." There weren't too many words of encouragement that Spring could offer up right then.

"Look, I have two weeks to come up with seven hundred stacks for Benny, or the only other option is to go to war with him. I hope you got some ideas 'cause Corey is freaking out right now."

Spring never told her about the armored truck heist because she didn't think that Summer was ready for that, but after sitting in front of her today, it was obvious that she was.

"Well, I have something big planned, and it's sure to cover the seven hundred thousand and then some. Follow my instructions and you'll never have to worry about money again."

Summer scooted up to the edge of her seat, tuned in, and listened to Spring's game plan. When Summer left the jail, she went straight to Corey's house. Everything Spring told her needed to go into effect immediately. There was little to no time to waste if the truck heist was going to become a reality.

When she finally pulled up to Corey's house, Summer was somewhat impressed with Corey's taste. His house was in a suburban neighborhood and on his street was little to no traffic. The house itself looked nice, and he even had the nerve to have a rose garden on the side of his house.

Summer rang the bell, and when Corey came down-stairs and opened the door, he looked at Summer with confusion.

"Why didn't you just use ya key?" he asked then turned around and walked back into the house.

Summer followed him, cursing Spring out in her head for not telling her about the keys. "I left them at home," Summer said. Looking around his house and not paying attention, she ran right into him as he stood in the dining room.

"Are you all right? You act like you never been here before." He wrapped his arms around her. "Damn, I couldn't wait to get you alone."

He leaned in to kiss her, and she had to admit the way that he kissed her was mind blowing and making her hot. She didn't mind playing Spring's role when it came to that.

"Come on, let's go upstairs," Corey said. He backed Summer up the steps with a few kisses.

Now, kissing was one thing, but Summer could tell that Corey was trying to get some pussy. Second base was as far as she was willing to go with him. There was no way Spring would be okay with Summer going too much further with her man.

"Wait, I gotta explain the plan to you," Summer said in between kisses in hopes she could get him to stop.

Corey was already in the zone. "Yeah, tell me all about it." He took off his T-shirt on his way up the steps.

He looked like something out of a *Men's Health* mag-azine. His stomach was ripped to the core, his chest had definition to it, and his arms were pretty well toned. His many tattoos made the whole package look sexy as hell.

Oh my God, I can't give my sister's man my goodies! Summer thought when Corey lifted her off her feet and wrapped her legs around his waist.

"Wait, we can't—"

Corey engulfed her mouth with his before she could even finish her sentence.

He walked her to the bedroom and laid her on the bed. In Summer's mind, she wanted him to stop, but her body was saying something else. He leaned in and kissed her again, then popped open her blouse so he could taste her bare skin. Summer moaned the farther down south he went. When he got to her stomach, he reached down, grabbed her jeans, and began to yank them off. Once they were on the floor, he removed her panties. Summer tried to stop his hands from pulling her panties off, but she was so flustered she didn't have much strength to stop him.

"I missed this pussy," Corey said.

He kissed the center of her sweetness then bit down on her pussy like a Georgia peach, French kissing and licking all over her box.

Summer threw her head back. She couldn't believe how good Corey made her feel. She'd had her pussy eaten before, but never like this.

Spring is going to kill me! This wasn't supposed to be happening, but she was so wrapped up in how good it felt that she didn't have the will power to stop it.

Corey unhooked her bra and tossed it to the side, exposing her chest to the air. Her nipples became rock hard and sensitive to the touch, so when Corey reached up and pinched them, Summer climaxed instantly. She held on to the back of his head with both hands, rocking back and forth as her orgasm reached its peak.

"Oh, yes, oh, yeah, right there right there," Summer yelled as cum splashed all over Corey's face.

Summer ripped the sheets off the bed from the tongue-lashing. When she finally came to, Corey was lying on top of her looking down into her eyes. He didn't say or do anything. He just looked into her eyes. Summer was waiting for him to break the seal and push his dick into her, but he didn't. He just kept staring at her, from her eyes to her chest and then down to her stomach.

He thought that he was tripping out until he got down to her feet. The mole on her foot wasn't there. He looked back up to her eyes, and Summer pulled her foot away from him, just about giving herself up. It was at that very moment Corey knew that he wasn't tripping. He leaned in as if he was about to kiss her, and at the same time he grabbed his gun off the nightstand. Summer felt the cold steel pressed against her face, and for a split second she thought that she was dead.

"Who da fuck are you and where the fuck is Spring?" Corey asked with malice in his eyes.

The jig was up and it was now time for Summer to come clean before she got herself killed.

Spring looked out of her cell door and could see her cell mate looking up at the TV. Karan glanced over and waved for Spring to come over because the news was on. That's the only thing Spring would watch.

"This shit happened around your way," Karan said, pointing up to the TV screen. The police were taking a dead body out of Cobbs Creek Park. The news anchor refused to say the name of the victim, but Spring was well aware of who it was. She smiled at the thought of her sister being one of the last people he saw before he died. She didn't pull the trigger, but that was cool. For all Vick knew, Spring was the one who took his life, and she was good with that.

Corey sat in the chair on the other side of the room while Summer sat on the edge of the bed fixing her hair. Corey was still trying to process everything that Summer had told him about being Spring's twin sister. He was baffled and at a loss for words.

"So how long have you . . ." He paused, still shocked at how much Summer looked like Spring.

"When she got locked up, the judge never gave her bail. Two homicide detectives had been investigating her for Trey and Mac's deaths, and just recently, a double homicide at the Orange facility."

Corey had an even more confused look on his face. "A double homicide? Why didn't she just call me and tell me?"

"My sister didn't tell you because she didn't want you to get hurt. She knew that once y'all found out that she was locked up and wasn't coming home anytime soon, things would get even crazier out here. Benny showed up at my mother's house and threatened her. I know he would have been coming for you and me next." Summer got up from the bed to look at herself in the mirror.

"Yeah, and I would have killed Benny and his boys," Corey said. "Fuck dem niggas. I go hard too."

Summer looked somberly at Corey's reflection in the mirror. "And that's exactly why she didn't call you." If it weren't for the choices Spring made by letting Summer take her place, Corey would have already been dead.

"So now what? I mean, how do you plan on coming up with 700K in two weeks?" Corey asked.

Summer finished up her hair and took a seat on the edge of the bed in front of him. "From what Spring told me, we're supposed to be takers. So, let's take some shit."

Detectives Keys and Allen escorted one of the cops from the Washington Avenue shootout to the morgue to view Vick's remains. The cop walked over to the cold steel table and quickly identified Vick as the shooter who shot his partner and almost took his life in the process. He couldn't even stand there, thinking about his partner who was still on life support.

"Excuse me," the officer said. He tilted his hat to the detectives before walking out.

Keys and Allen stood above Vick, looking at his body. "Whoever did this to him really messed him up bad," Keys said.

"One thing we know for sure is that Spring couldn't have done this. I tell you one thing, God must be on her side. This case we were starting to build on her is beginning to deteriorate. We gotta come up with something on that Mac and Trey case or she'll be getting out of that as well," Keys said with irritation.

He and Detective Allen left the morgue in search of some new clues that could help their case against Spring.

Chapter 14

Summer and Corey sat in his car waiting for Gary to get off so they could talk to him. She looked over at Corey and couldn't help but ask, "How did you know that I wasn't my sister?"

Corey took his eyes off the building for a split second to look over at her. "You don't wanna know the answer to that."

Summer didn't want to know; she needed to know. Until then, the only person able to tell them apart was her mother. "No, I . . . I really do," Summer insisted. "What gave me away?"

Corey sat there for a moment thinking about it. "I've known ya sister for a few years now, and during that time I have come to know just about everything about her physical appearance. I know her moves, her sounds. For instance, she doesn't scream when we have sex. She takes it like a big girl. And her taste is different than yours. It's like eating apples and peaches."

"Well, that was a lot of information." Summer waved him off.

"Nah, let me finish. At first, I really didn't notice it. You probably could have gotten away with it if it had been nighttime and the lights were out. When I scanned ya body, three things stuck out to me. Ya breasts are slightly larger than hers. I knew that from the size of ya areola. It's wider in diameter. Ya sister also has a mole on her right foot, which you don't have. But the main thing that gave you away is when I look into ya eyes," Corey said and then paused.

"What, what about my eyes?" Summer pressed.

"When I look into ya eyes I don't feel anything."

"Now you're starting to confuse me. Please enlighten me."

"I didn't feel anything because there's no love between me and you. When I'm with ya sister, it's always something special." Corey smiled, thinking about Spring. "You wouldn't understand."

Summer sat there quietly, amazed at how a man could be so observant about the person he was sleeping with. The love that he and Spring had was stronger than what Spring had explained. She didn't know why her sister felt the need to hide it from her. But it was her business, and sometimes it was good to keep some things to yourself.

"Pick ya head up. He just walked out of the building," Corey said and started his car.

Pushing up on Gary in front of his job wouldn't be a good look. But as soon as the opportunity presented itself, it was on.

Lou woke up after taking a quick cat nap. The first thing he laid eyes on when he sat up in the bed was the book bag Spring had given him from his dad. He knew there was money inside, but he never opened it to see how much.

"Let me see something," he mumbled to himself.

He got up and grabbed the bag then sat back down. After unzipping the bag, he dumped all the contents out on the bed. It definitely was a lot of money. Also, there was a white envelope and a Glock 9 mm. He picked the gun up and examined it, popping the clip out to see if a bullet was in the chamber. It was fully loaded with one in the head, nothing less than what Lou expected of his father.

The envelope was sealed, and when Lou opened it, there was a letter from his dad. At first he wasn't going to read it right away, knowing that these were the last words of his father. Without prolonging it, he decided to get it over with.

Wassup son,
If you got this letter, that means shit went bad for ya old man. I hope Spring was strong enough to deliver this bag to you personally, but knowing her and how much she loves you, she probably wasn't able to. So tell Corey I said thanks.

Lou had to smile at how sharp his pop was.

But anyway, I'ma keep this letter as short as possible in the hope that I leave a big impact on you. First, if you picked this letter up before anything, that means you have a good heart, much like ya mom. I would encourage you to go off to college and make something of yourself and live a righteous life to the best of ya ability. Now, if you picked the money up before anything else that means you like money and more than likely you gon' be a drug dealer. If that's the case, then here's enough bread to get you in the game. Just make sure that you keep ya circle tight and be ten steps ahead of the feds. They're always watching. Now if you picked up the gun before anything else, that means you a chip off the old block. You know I take money, and if that's in the future for you, always keep a bullet in the chamber and never go against ya gut instinct.
In the bag is 100K. If you can turn what's in the bag into 500K, then I can put you on to a score

that will sit you down for the rest of your life. You will never have to worry about money a day in ya life and ya children's children will still eat from it after you're dead and gone. When you get 500K, you call this number: 215-555-8820. Caesar will be expecting ya call. Other than that, I want you to know that I love you, son, more than anything in this world. And if you ever feel alone, know for sure that I'm looking down on you. Shit, knowing all the fucked-up shit I did in my life, I might be looking up from hell. LOL. In any event, I'll be there with you in spirit.

Take care, son.

Lou folded the letter and bit back his tears. He breathed deeply and nodded his head. Placing the letter back where he found it, he laughed. Even from the grave, his dad was still a father.

Corey followed Gary unnoticed, waiting for the right time to pull him over. It had begun to rain so it couldn't be just anywhere.

"Roll ya window down," Corey instructed Summer. He pulled around one car then pulled up right beside Gary.

Gary looked over and let out a frustrated sigh, then waited until they got to the light to roll down his window.

"Follow me!" Corey yelled out to him.

"For what?" Gary shouted back with an attitude.

Corey didn't even answer him. He just pulled off into traffic. Gary didn't want to, but he did what he was told and followed him. Corey pulled under an overpass, not too far from the highway and out of the rain. Gary pulled in right behind him.

"A'ight, look, he only deals wit' you—well, with Spring—so you're on ya own," Corey informed Summer before they got out of the car.

"Yo, y'all had your chance and you fucked up," Gary said as soon as he exited his car.

"Come on wit' all the tough-guy shit," Summer checked him quickly. "You know sometimes shit happens, but you know I'm good now."

"Yeah, I heard about ya boy, Vick. Nigga tried to pay me to do the job, but I shot him down. All money ain't good money, ya dig? Plus, I was only fuckin wit' you and Trey on this one."

"A'ight, so give me the time and the date," Summer said.

Gary looked over at Corey and then back into Summer's eyes. "You got my money?"

"What's the least you'll take right now as a down payment? I know it was three hundred stacks, but I'm telling you right now that I don't have that kind of money right at this moment."

"Well, you don't wanna do the job," Gary said, ready to end the whole conversation. "I told you what the sting is worth and, plus, I'm risking too much as it is. Three hundred thousand is the least I can do for this job."

"I got half of it."

"I can't do it. It's either all or nothing."

"Look at me. I'll give you my word that when the gig is done I'll pay you the rest of the money and I'll throw in an extra one hundred thousand just for you looking out for me."

Gary could look into her eyes and see that she was sincere, and though his gut was telling him that he could trust her, he still wanted his money.

"Meet me right here, Sunday at two o'clock. And bring two hundred thousand with you. After the job, I want three hundred more. That's the best I can do for you," Gary spoke sternly.

Summer held out her hand to seal the deal, and after shaking it, Gary walked back to his car. Just like that, the heist was on again.

Spring couldn't believe it when her name was called out for mail call. She hadn't been there that long, and not many people knew that she was locked up.

"It's legal mail, so you gotta sign for it," Karan told Spring when she made it through the crowd.

It was a letter from McMan, telling her that she had a bail hearing in two weeks. It was the best that he could do with the courts being jam-packed. He also noted that he would be up there to see her on the weekend to discuss trial strategies for the two gun cases.

"Shit, girl, you gotta try to get out on house arrest or something. Since ya case ain't that serious, you're eligible for it," Karan explained.

House arrest sounded better than being in jail. Spring was losing weight by the day, and the cell walls were starting to take a toll on her. She didn't see how females like Karan, who had been in for over a year, could still have their sanity. It was the same routine every single day. Like a broken record. The only thing Spring was looking forward to was the visit. House arrest didn't sound that bad at all.

"Ay, Spring . . . I mean, whatever ya name is."

"My name is Summer," she corrected Corey.

"Okay, Summer, as of late all you've been doing is making a lot of financial promises to everyone. I really hope you got some money in the trunk or something," Corey said as he drove. "You know that we only got twenty-five thousand off of Vick when we found him and, as far as I know, me and Spring put up our last before Vick came and stole that shit. The point is, we broke."

Summer shushed Corey, unable to get her thoughts together on how she planned to pull a rabbit out of her hat. Spring and Summer had already discussed things, and Spring had come up with a brilliant plan for how they'd get everything to fall into place. She reached into her bag and dug around until she found the game changer. It was the phone that Luv had given Spring the day she went and got the twenty-four bricks for Mike. She put one finger up to her mouth to shush him one more time before she pushed call. It rang a few times before Luv finally answered.

"Damn, I was wondering when or if I would ever get this call," Luv said when he answered "Tell me, to what do I owe this pleasure?"

"Well, I was wondering if we could go and get a bite to eat, and maybe even have ourselves a drink or two. Maybe even start a bar fight." Summer giggled.

"Well, I'm in the air right now on my way to Miami. I won't be back in the city until tomorrow afternoon. You think you'll be free for lunch?" Luv asked.

Summer was a pro at the cat and mouse game and knew that if she played it well she'd have Luv wrapped around her finger in no time. "I'm gonna have to take a rain check. You're not the only one who's busy. I'll call you back whenever my schedule becomes free," Summer said then hung up the phone before giving Luv a chance to respond.

"What the hell was all that about?" Corey asked.

She looked over at him and smiled. "Don't worry. We'll have that money by Sunday. That's my word," she said then sank into her seat.

"It's all circumstantial evidence, and I wish that there was enough to take to the grand jury, but there isn't enough," the District Attorney told Detectives Keys and Allen as they stood in her office. "If you guys want me to bring charges, you're going to have to get more. Otherwise, she's going to walk."

Keys and Allen walked out of her office with their tails tucked between their legs. They both had heard the bail hearing that Spring would have in the next couple of weeks. The word through the grapevine was that she going to get a bail. One that was sure to be posted immediately.

"So, now what?" Detective Allen smacked an elevator button. The DA's news had definitely thrown them for a loop.

"I guess we have to start from the beginning and comb through every piece of evidence we have. See if we've missed something, you know. I can tell you one thing that I know for sure. Spring Stewart had something to do with each and every one of those killings, and sooner rather than later it's going to come to the light," Keys stated before getting on the elevator.

The DA's choice was a blow to both of them. They felt sure that they had their suspect, but there was nothing they could say or do to bring her to justice at this point in time. Allen didn't want to admit it, but starting over only meant that they'd hit a brick wall.

Chapter 15

Summer sat in the visiting room with her dark shades on, waiting for Spring to come out. She shook her head when she noticed one of the male guards smiling at her. For a minute, she thought that he was about to come from around the booth and try to talk to her.

"Damn, girl, you out here looking like you the leader of the Black Panthers with those shades on," Spring joked when she came from the back. "Get ya lazy ass up and give me a hug."

Summer smiled and hugged her sister. "Shit, it's been a rough couple of days. I swear I can't see how you do it. Oh, and by the way, Corey knows about me."

Spring's jaw dropped to the ground. She had to make sure that she heard her right, so she told Summer to repeat it.

"Yeah, he knows everything, and had I not told him, I probably wouldn't be standing here right now." Summer chuckled, thinking about how he had reacted that day.

"Oh, my God, how did he—"

Summer cut her off. The image of Corey licking between her legs jumped into her mind. "I don't think you wanna know the answer to that."

"Yes, the hell I do," Spring insisted.

"Let's just say, that man is in love with you and knows every intricate detail about ya body, all the way down . . ."

Summer paused for a second, not wanting to go in too deep, for fear of how Spring may really feel about him. "All the way down to the mole on ya right foot."

Spring covered her mouth with her hand, shocked that he'd paid that much attention to it. She then cut her eyes over at Summer, wondering how far she and Corey had gone.

"Tell me you didn't sleep with him." Spring smacked Summer's leg. To be honest, Spring was a little anxious to know.

"Girl, ain't nobody sleep with that boy. You know I don't give my goodies up like you. But I have to admit I did let him taste it though." Summer stayed quiet and waited for her sister's reaction.

"You did what?" The way Spring reacted, it was hard to tell if she was pissed off or genuinely surprised.

"Okay, calm down! I tried to stop him, but everything happened so fast. Before I knew it, he was down there. But don't worry. It meant nothing to him." Summer quickly tried to lighten the situation.

"Really? And how do you know that?" Spring questioned.

"Because he put a gun to my head the second he realized I wasn't you. That, and, he said that when he looked into my eyes, he didn't see the love there."

Spring threw her head back and laughed. She'd never heard Corey sound so sensitive.

"Stop laughing. You telling me that you don't love him back?"

"I'm just going to say that it's complicated. Anyways, tell me what's going on with Luv. Did you meet up with him yet?"

"Tomorrow we're supposed to have lunch. I can tell by the way he talks that he was really feeling you. It shouldn't be that hard for me to get in, do what I gotta do, and get out," Summer said with confidence.

Summer made it seem like she couldn't understand how Spring managed to live such a wild life, but Spring could tell that Summer was actually starting to like it.

"A'ight, sis." Spring raised her eyebrow. "This is make it or break it. So don't fuck up."

"Santana," Benny yelled from the restaurant's kitchen.

Santana left the conversation he was having with a female and walked to the back. Benny was standing at the cutting table, chopping up some vegetables he was about to use for the meal.

"You know, I was thinking about what that piece of shit told us before I killed him. That heist is worth a lot of money," Benny said as he continued prepping his food.

It's funny because Santana couldn't seem to get that off his mind either. He'd slept on it all night, imagining what he could do with that kind of money.

"Yeah, *papi,* so what are you saying?"

"I'm saying, you might get a couple of the guys and muscle in on that lick. What do you think? You think you can handle something like that?"

Santana had done his fair share of home invasions, knocking off corner hustlers and maybe even a bodega or two in his time. But he'd never robbed anything as big as a bank or an armored truck. He wasn't scared at all. In fact, he got a little adrenaline rush just thinking about it.

"Yeah, boss, I can handle that," he told Benny.

Benny put a large piece of flounder in the pan along with the vegetables, and a few sprinkles of seasonings. His cooking process was delicate. Something like an

Italian mobster, except Spanish music played in the background.

"Just so we're clear, it's being split straight down the middle. That's $1.9 million apiece, give or take a couple hundred grand," Benny explained. "Can you handle all of that money?" Benny smiled, knowing that it would be the first time Santana had a million dollars of his own.

"Yeah, I can handle it," Santana shot back.

"A'ight, get rid of ya little girlfriend, sit down, and have dinner wit' me so we can discuss business."

Summer turned her phone on as soon as she got into the parking lot of the jail. It wasn't more than a minute later that the phone rang. It was Corey.

"Wassup, Summer?"

"I just got out of the county," she answered. "Where are you?"

"I'm at Lou's house. Come through because we need to talk," he said and gave her the address.

Summer started up the Range Rover. It sounded a little urgent so she got there as quick as she could. When she pulled up in front of Lou's house, Lou and Corey were sitting out on the front steps smoking weed.

"This shit better be important. I got a manicure appointment at three-thirty," Summer said as she walked up the driveway.

"Yeah, this might be a little more important than a manicure," Lou said. He jumped up and led Summer into the house.

As she walked up the steps, she looked over at Corey, who was still sitting there. "Does he know about me?" she whispered.

Corey shook his head no. At first he wanted to tell him, but he didn't feel that it was his place to do so.

"So, Corey told me that we needed some money to secure the armored truck job," Lou said. He led Summer into the kitchen.

"Yeah, we're missing like one hundred and eighty thousand," she replied.

When she got into the kitchen, on the table was a pile of money.

"Did you know?" Lou asked.

Summer didn't know what to say. He was under the impression that he was talking to Spring. The truth was, Summer didn't know what he was talking about.

"Lou, I have to tell you something that's very important, so I think we should sit down."

She didn't want to lie to him anymore. Lou and Corey were the closest people to Spring outside of Summer and her mother. It seemed like Lou and Corey loved Spring just as much. Summer looked at Lou and smiled at the curious look on his face.

"This is going to be a bit of a shock, but I'll answer any questions you may have afterward because I know you'll have plenty."

"Hold on, what the hell is going on?" Lou was now a little concerned.

Summer took in a deep breath. "I'm not who you think I am. My real name is Summer. I'm Spring's twin sister."

Lou looked at her for a moment then started to laugh. At that moment, Corey walked into the house and headed to the kitchen.

"Ay, yo, Spring smoking that shit," Lou joked.

"Lou, I'm for real." Summer placed her hand on top of his.

He looked into her eyes and could tell that she was serious.

"Corey, tell Lou who I really am," Summer said, all the while looking at Lou.

"Her name is Summer. That's Spring's twin sister, li'l homie," Corey informed him and took a seat at the table.

Lou's face went blank, then a hint of anger appeared. He pulled his hand away from Summer then put the money back onto the pile. "Prove it," Lou demanded, still in a state of disbelief. He couldn't fathom the thought of it being true, especially since he felt he knew Spring better than most.

"It's true, li'l homie. Spring's locked up in the county right now. I called early this morning," Corey confirmed.

"You gotta be fuckin' kidding me," Lou snapped and got up from the table.

Summer tried to grab his arm before he could walk off, but he snatched it away from her then stormed out of the house.

"Just leave him alone for a minute. He'll be all right," Corey said.

Detective Keys looked up at his bulletin board and took in a deep breath. He had pictures of Trey, Mac, Spring, Mike, Vick, and the two Spanish guys who were killed at the storage company. Pictures of the evidence that was recovered from each crime were posted up at their respective scenes. He had been staring at the pictures for over an hour now, trying to bring something to life. He needed to come up with something before Parker reassigned him to another case.

"Hey, David," Patricia, a narc detective, spoke when she walked up behind him. "Mark told me to drop this off to you." She passed him a manila envelope. She was about to walk off when she noticed one of the people in the pictures.

"What did Gordo do now?" she asked and pointed to one of the Spanish guys who was killed at the storage company.

Keys took his eyes off the board for the first time in a little under an hour. "You know this guy?"

"Yeah, he's from the north side. I think he's still running with Benny."

"Who the hell is Benny?" Keys asked. He cracked open the manila envelope and looked at the warrants to search Vick's house.

Patricia gave him a quick rundown on who Benny was and the major role he played in the heroin game that plagued the city. She had been on his case for a year before her supervisor snatched her and the rest of her unit off the case.

"Why were you reassigned from the case?"

"Word is, the feds picked it up," Patricia said and walked off.

Detective Keys sat there in deep thought, looking at Gordo's pictures. His thought process went into overdrive. The case was starting to come together just a little. Another piece had been added to it, which he was sure to investigate.

Summer walked out onto the porch where Lou was rolling up a blunt. She took a seat next to him, hoping that he wouldn't get up. "Please don't be mad at me. And definitely don't be mad at Spring," Summer began.

Lou stayed quiet, putting some fire to the blunt then taking a deep drag.

"You have to understand that there was a reason why she did it."

"Yo, I'm not even mad," Lou said. "I trust that whatever reason Spring had for not telling me about you was for the best. I guess I just feel some type of way because she didn't trust me enough to tell me, you know. She's like my big sister. I trust her with my life," Lou said. He looked over at Summer then took another toke. "Damn, you look just like her," he said, shaking his head.

Summer smiled, reached over, and took the blunt out of his hand. "Well, we are twins," she said.

She took a small puff of the blunt. The weed filled her lungs and, as she attempted to exhale, she began to cough uncontrollably. That was the first time she'd ever smoked weed. Spit came out of her mouth, snot ran from her nose, and tears fell from her bloodshot eyes.

"Yeah, you got those virgin lungs." Lou chuckled. "Gimme my shit back!" He laughed while Summer continued to smoke.

Corey came out to the porch at the tail end of it, and by the time Summer looked up at him, she was already high.

"That shit is too strong," she complained with her eyes low.

Corey had to laugh at her himself.

"So what's good? What are we going to do about this money?" Lou asked. He looked over at Summer with a serious face. "No more secrets, and I want ya word on that."

"I give you my word that there will be no more secrets. Not from me or from Spring," Summer promised.

That's all Lou needed to hear. "Let's put my pop's money to good use."

"Yeah, but we still short about eighty grand," Corey cut in.

They both looked over at Summer, who was still trying to get her marbles. The weed was taking its toll on her, but she was well aware of what she needed to do.

"That should be a piece of cake. I'm supposed to have lunch with my mark tomorrow. Just make sure we got extra clips and vests by the end of the week," Summer said.

Time was moving fast, and next week was going to be the present in a flash. There were so many things that needed to be done before the heist went down, all to ensure the success of it. Summer was going to make sure that the plan Spring had for the job would be executed to the letter, and the number one goal and main priority was to make sure everyone made it out alive.

Chapter 16

Summer pulled up to the bistro where Luv had planned their lunch date. It was nice, and probably a little bit over the top. She did manage to come out of her street clothes, which consisted of jeans and sneakers. Today, she had on a white wraparound sundress and some tan and brown leather Jimmy Choo sandals, courtesy of Spring's closet. Her hair was straight down, passing by her shoulders, and on her arm was a tan Prada bag.

"You don't have to stare at me," Summer said when she walked up to the table Luv had already reserved. Based on how empty the place was, it seemed that he had reserved the whole place.

"You make it hard for me not to stare." He stood up to hug her.

Luv pulled out Summer's chair for her then popped the cork off a bottle of red wine. He poured just the right amount in a glass. Not enough to get her drunk, but enough for Summer to enjoy.

"Oh, I see you pulling out all the stops today," Summer said, admiring his mannerisms. "Is this how you work all the ladies?"

"Look at me, do it look like I need to charm a female? I only try to impress if I like," he said, giving Summer full eye contact.

Luv was a handsome man. Dark chocolate, wavy hair cut low, a full, thick beard, broad shoulders, and a nice muscular frame. His white cotton V-neck T-shirt showed off parts of his ripped chest. The scent of Gucci Guilty came from his body, and when he spoke, his voice was deep but soothing to the ear.

"So, let me ask you something. Why would somebody like you be off in the streets?" Luv said.

"What do you mean by that?"

"I mean with your looks and your brains, you should be doing something better with ya life."

"I wouldn't consider what I do to be a waste."

"If you picked up twenty-five bricks of dope for a nigga like Benny, yeah, I'd say what you're doing with your time is a waste."

"So what do you suggest?"

"I think you should marry me, pick out a house any-where in the world, and call it our home." Luv smiled.

"You wouldn't know the first thing to do with me, boy." Summer couldn't help the smile that crept to her lips. "Plus, you don't even know me. I could cut your throat in your sleep or something. Or blow all of your money and skip town."

"I know enough to know that you wouldn't do that. And to be honest wit' you, I think you're the most beautiful woman I've ever laid eyes on. I know for sure that if I had somebody like you lying in my bed at night, I'd go through hell and high water to make it home day after day. You would have no worries."

"And you got that from the two encounters that we've had?" Summer raised her eyebrow.

"Do you really find that hard to believe? Look at you. Have you listened to yourself speak?"

Summer was intrigued by the conversation, so much so that she almost forgot the reason she was there. Luv had a way with words and he seemed intelligent, unlike most of the men Summer seemed to attract. The scary part about it was that he sounded genuine.

This setup was going to be a little more difficult than what she'd thought, but Summer was definitely up for the challenge.

Gary walked through the aisle of the supermarket with his fiancée, laughing and playing around while they grocery shopped.

"You gon' eat that right now?" Gary asked when Kelsey popped the top on some butter pecan ice cream.

"Yeah, your son is hungry." She smiled and poked out her round stomach. "So, I saw a nice four-bedroom house in Phoenix, and it has a nice-sized backyard."

Gary sighed. The topic of conversation for the past three months had been about moving to Arizona. Kelsey had been offered a job there in hospital administration. With health benefits and bonuses, the pay would be in the six figures. Not only was the pay going to be good, Kelsey and Gary both had family in Arizona who wanted them to move there. Gary really didn't want to leave the city, but he agreed to move, just to support and make Kelsey happy. He didn't even have a job lined up, and that was mainly the reason why he'd planned the armored truck heist. He wanted to make sure that he and Kelsey would be set, at least for the first year or so.

"Baby, listen to me," Gary said, stopping Kelsey in the middle of the aisle. "You and my son mean the world to me, but I just want to make sure that we're straight when we move. Let me finish out the rest of the month and then we can go down there and look at a couple of houses."

Kelsey knew that she'd been putting pressure on Gary to move, but that was only because she knew that he had the potential to change his mind. She'd wanted out of the drug-infested neighborhood they'd lived in for way too long.

"I just want our son to grow up and have a chance. I want to leave this city behind and start over."

"I'm with you, baby. Just lighten up on me a little." Gary chuckled and lifted her chin so she'd look him in his eyes. "Can you do that for me, babe? Pleaassseee?"

Kelsey smiled and nodded. She knew that her hormones were playing a part in why she was nagging so much, but by no means was she about to stop looking for a house to move into. When the day came for them to roll out, she wanted to be ready.

"Girl, you got a visitor," Karan said when she walked into the room.

Spring, who was staring out the window, figured that it was her mother coming to get the one-on-one visit so she could finish grinding her up. Spring washed her face and put her hair in a ponytail then shot to the officers' booth.

"You go to court next week, don't you?" the female guard asked, trying to be friendly.

"Yeah, and I hope they let my ass out of here."

"I'll pray for you, girl. God knows that jail is not for women," she said and gave Spring her pass.

When she got to the visiting room, she looked around for her mom but she wasn't there. Then a familiar voice yelled out her name, making the hairs on the back of Spring's neck stand up. She had a feeling that one day Corey was going to pop up, and there he was sitting in the back looking like he wanted to chew her head off. She didn't know why, but an air of humility and submission came over her.

Spring walked up to him with her head down. Corey lifted her head up and looked into her eyes. "Are you all right?" he asked as he took her into his arms. His touch had never felt better, and Spring had to hold back the tears.

"I'm sorry that I didn't tell you."

Corey stopped her, letting her know that she didn't need to explain. His reasons for being there were strictly because he wanted to see her, touch her, and get as many kisses as he could from her. He wanted to talk to her about something other than the obvious drama that was going on out there on the streets.

In a sense, Spring wanted the same, and she thought about what Summer had told her about how much Corey loved her. She'd had more than enough time to think about it, and she finally came to the conclusion that she loved Corey more than she'd thought. If allowed, she was going to take the time out today to let him know all the reasons why.

"I really enjoyed having lunch with you today," Summer said, walking next to Luv as she was leaving.

"Likewise. Now I just have to see if I can get another date out of you."

Summer never had a guy who liked her as much as he did. Not just that, but Luv was willing to go out on a limb to prove it. It was attractive, but Summer had to stick to the number one rule Spring had given her, which was not to catch feelings for the mark.

"How about we have dinner at your place tomorrow night?" Summer suggested.

"You tell me when and where you want me to pick you up. We can definitely make that happen," Luv assured her.

Just then, Lou pulled up in the Range Rover. He stepped out and stood at the door, putting up a front that he was her driver.

"How about I text you with my address tomorrow?" Summer said as she slowly backed up to her car.

Luv had a couple of things to do tomorrow night, but he wasn't about to miss out on having dinner with who he thought was Spring. "I'll be waiting," Luv said before Summer disappeared into the car.

"How about Alex?" Kelsey asked as they walked to the car with the groceries.

"Alex sounds too white," Gary responded and made a face.

He was about to give her a few names he'd thought of but paused once he saw a man leaning against his car.

"Yo, my man, that's me," Gary announced as they approached.

"Yeah, I know," the man said. "I need to have a word with you, Gary, if you don't mind."

"Who the fuck are you and how do you know my name?" Gary said and pulled Kelsey close to him.

The man turned to the side so Gary could see the gun on his waist. Gary matched him, lifting his shirt up so the man could see the gun in the holster on his waist.

"Come on, Gary, not in front of the mother of your unborn child," he advised. "I just want to talk. Let's not make a scene."

Kelsey looked nervously from Gary to the man, wondering what was going on. Gary noticed the look in the man's eyes and could tell that it was something important.

"K, get in the car," Gary told her. When she did, he leaned up against the door to see what he wanted.

"To answer your question, my name is Benny. I'm not gonna beat around the bush with you. Vick put me on to the sting and I'm trying to get in on it," Benny said bluntly.

"Look, homie, I don't know what Vick told you, but I'm not—"

"The chick isn't going to come up with the money. She's broke as hell, running around trying to scrape up the money. I have three hundred stacks for you right now, plus an extra two hundred after the job is done. Now, from what I understand, that's a lot more than what she can come up with if she can come up with anything at all."

Gary sat there weighing the pros and cons, trying to figure out what to do. In his mind, Spring had been bullshitting ever since Trey checked out, and it wasn't a guarantee that she was going to come through this time. Gary was becoming fascinated with the score. It was something he had to go through with, even if Spring wasn't in on it.

"You said you already have the money?" Gary asked.

"It's already in your trunk with a prepaid cell phone I'll call you on later." Benny put out his fist for a bump to lock it in.

Gary thought about Kelsey and the baby, and everything they'd talked about. He really wanted to get it done and over with so they could get out of the city for good. Gary tapped Benny's fist with his, then jumped in his car and pulled out of the parking lot. It was on for sure now.

"What you over there smiling about?" Summer asked Lou as he was driving. "Still can't believe it, huh?'

Lou shook his head no. He couldn't tell them apart to save his life. She looked like Spring, talked like Spring, and her street smarts were beginning to equal up to Spring's.

"So, tell me about yourself," Lou requested.

Summer could understand that he wanted to know more about her, and at the same time, she wanted to know Lou better as well. Spring had always spoke highly of Lou and his dad.

"Me and my sister were very close growing up. Our mom used to dress us up in the same outfits and play mind games with her homegirls when we were younger," Summer began. "When we graduated from high school, I went to college to be a psychiatrist."

Interrupted by her phone, Summer stopped talking. The caller was listed as unavailable, which meant that more than likely it was Spring. Summer quickly accepted it.

"Hey, big head, we were just talking about you."

"Who, you and Mom?" Spring said.

"Nah, it's Lou with me. You wanna talk to him?"

"You told Lou too? You telling everybody now?" Spring barked.

"Calm down, Spring. Corey and Lou are the closest to you. It was only right for me to tell Lou." Summer pleaded her case.

"No, it isn't. Do you know what could happen if word gets out that you're not me?"

"Yes, Summer, I do, which is why I felt it was important to bring Lou up to date with what's going on." Summer continued, "Now that Lou and Corey know, they can help me out and step up if we get put in a situation I might not be prepared to handle."

Spring took a second to process what her sister was saying. She had to admit that Summer had a point. Lou was like family to her, and to keep a secret like that from him would be unfair. And with both Corey and Lou knowing that was her sister out there with them, they'd definitely keep a closer eye on her to make sure she stayed safe.

"You're right, Summer, but Lou and Corey are the only ones that can know about this," she said sternly into the phone.

"I understand, big sister," Summer replied. Spring was her big sister by one minute and twenty-nine seconds. Growing up, Spring always made sure to remind Summer of it.

"And don't you forget it!" Spring chuckled. "Tell Lou I'll get at him in a minute. First, I want to remind you that I go to court on the nineteenth so I'm going need bail money on deck. Plus, I need you to come up here tomorrow, too."

"A'ight, that's no problem. I'll be there."

"Cool. Now, put Lou on the phone. I know he's staring at you right now."

Summer couldn't help but to laugh when she looked over and saw Lou staring down her throat. Lou pulled the car over when she handed him the phone.

"I see you got all the sense."

"Yeah, I know. Please don't be mad at me, Lou. I'll explain everything to you when I get home."

"And when is that supposed to be? I really need to holla at you." Lou couldn't wait to tell Spring about the letter his dad left behind. She'd know just what to do and how to do it.

"How about you come up here with my sister tomorrow? I got a couple of things I wanna talk to you about as well. Does that sound like a plan?" Spring asked.

"I'll be there. Now let me get off this phone. I love you, big sis."

Spring's heart always melted when she heard Lou say that.

Chapter 17

Summer gave Luv the address to the hideout instead of Spring's real address. When he pulled up to the house, some of the neighbors who were still outside watched in awe as the Rolls-Royce Phantom came to a stop in front of the house. Luv was followed by a black Cadillac Escalade. It was his security. He was getting money for real. Definitely in the top five when it came to the richest men in the city.

"Oh, this nigga showing out," Corey said, peeking through the living room window.

Summer came down the stairs rocking a faux leather shirt, some Brian Atwood cow-skin stilettos, and a white V-neck T-shirt.

"How do I look?" she asked Lou when she got up to the door.

"Like ya sister." He chuckled. "Nah, but you good. Where's ya strap?"

Summer had a small chrome .25 automatic tucked away in her Gucci bag. Corey walked up to her, stood directly in front of her and looked right into her eyes.

"Are you ready?"

Summer nodded.

"A'ight, go ahead. Do ya thing and get out of there. If the nigga get crazy, don't hesitate to put a bullet in his head," Corey advised. "I'll be right up the street from y'all, so I'll come in guns blazin' if I have to."

"Don't worry about it, I got it," Summer assured him. Summer didn't want to have Luv waiting any longer, so she headed for the door.

"You look good," Luv said when he got out of the car. "You might fuck around and not come home tonight, looking this good."

Summer blushed. "You don't look that bad yourself."

Luv's cream linen pants and shirt blew in the wind. On his feet were a pair of cream croc-skin loafers and, as always, he had a fresh haircut with a clean line-up. If Luv wasn't a man she was planning to rob, he surely was the type of guy Summer wouldn't mind dating.

"Before we go anywhere, I have something that I need to take care of," Luv told Summer before pulling off.

"Do what you have to do. I know you're a busy man."

She figured that he had to make a few drop-offs and she didn't mind. Summer wanted him to feel like it was all about him, and as soon as he let his guard down well enough, she was going to strike. This was a one-shot deal, so whatever was going to happen had to happen tonight. It was a must that she succeed.

Lou went to his cousin Danny's house to buy a few items for the heist, as instructed by Summer. Danny had everything in the hood a nigga needed. With a dealer's license and the ability to make straw purchases, he was able to buy the best guns in bulk. Guns like FNS and baby Desert Eagles, compact AR-15s and more.

"Damn, li'l cuzzo, you picking out a lot of heavy shit!" Danny observed. "Who you about to go to war with, li'l nigga?"

"Man, I'm not going to war with anybody. I'm just trying to get my new crew right." Lou placed the Heckler and Koch on the table.

"Fuck, what y'all niggas about to rob a bank or some shit?"

"Cuz, you asking a lot of mafuckin' questions for a nigga who's about to make some money," Lou shot back. "Just give me a good price on all this shit right here."

Danny scanned the table. Lou had three Kevlar vests, six baby Desert Eagles, twelve extra clips, four boxes of bullets, and two compact AR-15s with two extra hundred-shot clips.

The items on the table had Danny a little worried. This wasn't like a distant cousin to him. They were first cousins, and the last thing he wanted was for something to happen to Lou.

"Lou, can we talk about this shit? I know we haven't had that much time to kick it after the funeral, but we can kick it now."

If Lou had any plans on leaving that house with all those guns, he had to give Danny something. "Look, cuz, I'm in the streets right now, and one thing my pops always told me was to always be prepared to go to war, even during times of ease. Like I told you, I got a li'l crew and we ain't taking any shorts out here on these streets. Now you can either be the solution for me to be able to protect myself out here in these streets or you can be the reason why a nigga can run up on me and put a bullet in the back of my head."

When Danny listened to the way Lou carried himself, he saw his uncle Trey in him. With Trey, safety was always first, and staying strapped at all times was his motto. Danny couldn't deny Lou, who was only a product of his bloodline.

"The ARs cost twelve hundred each, baby Desert Eagles four hundred each, vests are two hundred each, and the extra clips and bullets are free. So all together, for the family price, give me thirty-eight hundred and promise me you won't get yourself killed," Danny said. He dug into his pocket and pulled out an ounce of Grand Daddy Kush. "You can have this, too."

Lou went into his pocket and pulled out the money, hurried up and paid him, then bagged up the guns. He was trying to get the hell out of there before Danny changed his mind. Lou couldn't afford that. He had to take care of business.

"Where are we?" Summer asked, looking out of her window.

"Come on, you're about to find out," Luv said and got out of the car.

Summer got out of the car and looked up and down the street. The huge house looked like something that you would see on *MTV Cribs*. The other three houses on the block looked the same. Summer thought it was his house, until he had to ring the doorbell. About a minute later, an older woman with salt-and-pepper hair answered the door.

"Hey, Mom," Luv greeted her, giving her a big hug and a kiss on her cheek. Her gray hair was the only way to tell that she was up in age. Other than that, she had plenty of energy and looked young and vibrant.

"And who might this be?" she asked, stepping to the side so they could come in.

Luv walked ahead and took off up the steps. "That's my future," he yelled back down the stairs.

"Hi, my name is Spring," Summer introduced herself.

Luv's mother sized Summer up real good, checking her out from head to toe. It got to the point that Summer was starting to feel uncomfortable.

"You can call me Ms. Ann. You know, as long as I've known this boy, there's only one other female he brought to this house to meet me, and that was the mother of his child."

As soon as Ms. Ann said that, Luv came back down the stairs holding a sleeping toddler. He walked right up to Summer, who was standing side by side with Ms. Ann.

"Spring, I want you to meet my daughter, Ariana. Well, she's 'sleep right now, but she'll say hi to you one day." He smiled, looking down, and kissed the little girl on her forehead.

Summer's heart melted looking at the cute baby he was holding. She was so adorable, Summer wished that she could have bitten down on her fat little cheeks. Ms. Ann walked into the other room then came back with the baby's overnight bag.

"I'll see you on Monday," she said, playfully scooting everybody to the door.

"Yeah, we've been kicked out of better places." Luv laughed as he was leaving.

Ms. Ann held him back slightly while Summer walked out the front door. "She seems like a nice girl, but take it slow, baby," she said then hugged and kissed both Luv and Ariana.

He took that as her approval of who he thought was Spring, and that was something he needed before he went any further with her. He didn't know why, nor could he explain it, but Luv had it bad for her. From the moment they'd sat down for lunch the other day, he couldn't get his mind off of her. The last time he felt this way about somebody, that woman gave him some of the best years of his life.

"Karan, are you awake?" Spring asked from the top bunk.

"Girl, sleep is hard to come by around these parts," Karan answered and turned over on her side. "Why, what you up there thinking about?"

Spring had all kinds of shit picking at her brain. The main thing was Summer and how she was handling the whole Luv situation. She had faith and trust in her sister's abilities, but out there in those streets, anything was liable to happen. "I'm just up here thinking about life."

Spring was also thinking about Corey and the meaning-ful conversation they had on their visit the other day. She could see what Summer was talking about when Summer said that he loved her. He made it known how much he loved and missed Spring with words and actions. It had Spring thinking about letting him all the way in once she got home, public affection and the whole nine yards.

"I'm not gonna lie, girl. I'm down here thinking about all the time these people are trying to give me, and the fucked-up part about it is that the DA on my case is a female. That bitch act like she couldn't care less that the nigga was beating my ass every night. I should have just killed that nigga, stuffed his body in a suitcase, and threw his ass in a river somewhere," Karan vented.

Spring chuckled. "Damn, bitch, you crazy as hell. A suitcase, though?"

Karan laughed a little too, realizing how difficult the task would have been to pull off.

"When I get out of here, I'm coming back for you. I really could use somebody like you on my team, real talk."

"Now don't go making promises you can't keep. I've been in this jail for over a year and I done heard it all from the cellies who came and went."

"Trust me, you never had a celly like me before. When I give my word on something, best believe I see it through. Just make sure that when the time comes, you be ready."

They both lay in their beds thinking about the streets until they nodded off to sleep. Karan couldn't see it now, but her chances of coming up from under her current sit-uation were now greater than they'd ever been.

"So, did you figure out what you wanted to eat?" Luv asked when he walked into the kitchen where Summer sat patiently waiting.

She was still in awe of the beauty of his house. It wasn't as big as his mother's, but that was clearly by choice.

Even still, he had his pad looking plush. Hardwood floors, leather furniture, stainless steel appliances, and bright colors that lit up the place.

"Can I ask you something?" Summer asked, crossing her hands on the island.

"Go ahead."

"What happened to Ariana's mother? I noticed you don't talk about her much."

Luv opened the refrigerator and grabbed a bag of shrimp, along with a few other items. He knew that this question was going to be asked sooner or later. "I knew her since she was fourteen. Good girl, strong morals, and she was crazy about a sixteen-year-old dropout who liked to hang out on the corners."

"That was you, I'm assuming," Summer said as he continued to tell his story.

"Long story short, we got older, she got pregnant, and we were going to get married, but then she died giving birth," Luv explained as he prepared the food.

Summer put her hand over her mouth. She expected to hear a story about some deadbeat junkie, not that. "Oh, my goodness, I am so sorry," she said, wanting to get up and give him a hug.

"Nah, it's cool. That was a long time ago. I couldn't let it tear me apart 'cause I still needed to be a father. I'm all she got, and I have to be there for her."

Summer just sat there, not knowing what to say. She actually started to feel bad about what she was doing. Some people in this world deserved to get done to them what Summer was about to do; but, in her mind, Luv wasn't one of those people.

"So, what about you? What happened to your Mr. Right?" Luv asked as he put the shrimp into the pan.

"I don't know. I guess he's out there somewhere. I just haven't found him yet, nor am I in a rush. When he comes, he'll come, but one thing I'm not going to do is go out and look for him."

Luv didn't respond right away. He became focused on the food that he was cooking. Summer was curious as to what he was putting together, so she got up and walked over to the stove to see.

Steamed rice, extra-large shrimp, scallops, broccoli, diced carrots, and cauliflower. A small pan of buttered garlic sauce simmered on the back burner.

"Oh, let me find out you tryin' to show off," Summer said, nudging him on his side.

He was really putting his foot in it, too. Luv turned Summer around by her waist and walked her back over to the island. The food was just about done, and Summer was ready to eat.

"Just give me two more minutes," he requested and wiped his hands on the towel he had draped over his shoulder.

Summer sat there with a smile on her face, watching as he prepared the plates. She could honestly say that this was the first time a man had cooked for her, and tonight she was going to enjoy every moment of it.

Gary picked up the last stack of money from the duffle bag and was about to count it until he realized that there was no need to. He was already at $278,000, which was good enough for him. He reached over and grabbed the prepaid phone that was in the bag then dialed the number Benny had provided.

"'Bout time. I was about to put an APB out on ya ass," Benny answered, snapping his fingers at Santana for him to come over and listen to the conversation.

"What's good. Is this line secured?" Gary asked, looking at the stack of fifty dollar bills in his hand.

"You can talk freely," Benny assured him.

Gary sat up in his chair then took a deep breath. He began to break down the heist in detail, letting Benny know exactly how it needed to be executed. Times, locations, and everything else needed to be precise, and there was no room for error. The conversation lasted every bit of two and a half hours with Gary and Benny going over every worst-case scenario, and the most important part of the heist, which was the getaway. It was a plan that was foolproof and, if done correctly and exactly to a tee, there would be zero casualties on each side.

"Look, if you have any more questions or suggestions, just call me on this number," Benny told Gary, ready to end the call and to let everything marinate in his head.

Gary hung up the phone, and even if he wanted to, he couldn't turn back. The wheels were in motion and the only thing left to do was ride this thing out and then get out of dodge.

"Oh, my God, boy, you did that!" Summer praised as she wiped her mouth with her napkin. "I don't know how I'm going to top that."

Luv smiled, threw back the last swallow of wine, then got up from the table. "Come with me," he said and reached for her hand.

Summer got up from the table, wondering what else he had planned for this perfect night.

"I hope you know how to dance." He smiled as he walked her into the living room.

"Boy, don't nobody know how to dance," Summer responded, trying to pull away from him.

Luv pulled her back, grabbing one of the remote controls of the entertainment system at the same time. "Just hold on to me," he advised her and tossed the remote on the couch.

"Earned It" by The Weeknd softly played through the speakers.

Luv pulled Summer closer to him and wrapped his arms around her as they slowly drifted side to side. Summer's body fit snug against his, and she didn't know why, but the way he held her felt intoxicating.

Luv whispered the lyrics softly near her ear. She could feel his soft skin rubbing against her cheek. As she breathed deep, she could smell his cologne. Summer pulled her head back and looked into Luv's eyes as he looked back down into hers. The mood was set, and the atmosphere was right. It seemed like Luv had perfect timing. Leaning down, he softly pressed his lips against hers. He pulled back, looked into her eyes again, and this time, Summer reached up, grabbed the back of his head, and pulled his face back down to hers. She kissed him more passionately than the last time, and at this point, they both knew where this was going.

Luv took her by the hand and led Summer up the stairs. Her heart was racing a mile a minute. Her emotions were everywhere. She felt such a deep connection to this man and she wanted nothing more than to let him taste her and then feel him inside of her. But in that same instance, she felt like a traitor to her sister. This man was supposed to be her mark, not a love interest. She knew what was at stake if she messed this up, but she felt like she was dealing with a double-edged sword, and one way or another she was going to get stabbed.

She had only known this man for a few days, but when she looked into his eyes, she felt like she was home. She felt like she'd found something she never knew she'd lost. If she pulled away now, she could be turning her back on her first chance at love. Up until now, she had never met a man that made her feel the way Luv did. On the other hand, though, if she didn't go through with her sister's plans, it would cost a lot of lives, including her own.

Get it together, Summer! Stop kissing him! She tried
to pull away, but Luv placed his hands on the small of her
back and pulled her in tighter. She wasn't sure if it was
the wine kicking in or the fact that she was nervous as
hell, but her knees felt weak, and she felt herself surren-
dering to the sweet taste of his soft lips against her own.

His gentlemanly ways were still in full effect as he
softly lifted her up and placed her on his huge California
king bed. He peeled off his shirt and so did Summer. Her
skirt was next, but she kept her sandals on. Her pink
lace bra and boy shorts had Luv's dick bulging through
his pants. Summer looked so sexy; and just so he could
take in all of her beauty, he sat up between her legs and
rubbed his hands all over her body. Her skin was soft and
smooth, and Luv made a mental note of every inch of her.

"I have to tell you something," Summer whispered.

Luv slowly pulled her panties off and threw them to the
floor. "Let me find out on my own." He raised her leg and
kissed it from her calf to her thigh.

When he reached her treasure, he softly kissed it, too.
Summer was so zoned out, she didn't even notice that
he'd removed his pants and his boxers in one shot. She
threw her head back when he sucked and twirled his
tongue around her clit, causing Summer to become wetter and wetter. She could feel an orgasm about to come
on, but Luv couldn't wait another minute. He wanted to
be inside of her.

Climbing onto her, he grabbed a handful of his rock-
hard pole then rubbed the head of it up and down her wet
center. Summer hissed when he pushed the head of his
dick inside of her. She tried to relax her walls, but it did
no justice. Luv was blessed. Inch by inch, he dug deeper
inside of her. She moaned loudly, then bit down on his
shoulder. It hurt, but at the same time it felt good. His
slow, steady strokes opened Summer right up. She held

on to his back, digging her nails into his skin with every stroke. Summer looked up at Luv as he looked down at her. As they gazed into each other's eyes, a special connection was established.

She stuffed her tongue into his mouth as the passion between the two became more intense. On this night, she gave herself away to a man she hardly knew. It was exactly how she pictured it would be.

Chapter 18

After about an hour of driving around the unfamiliar neighborhood, Lou finally pinpointed Corey's location, on a side street not too far from Luv's house. Corey was leaning against his car when Lou pulled in behind him.

"Damn, this shit looks like Beverly Hills," Lou said, getting out of the car and looking around.

"Yeah, ol' boy live out here," Corey replied, giving Lou some dap.

"I been trying to call Summer all morning, but she's not answering."

"Something might be wrong, li'l homie." He took a puff of the weed then passed it to Lou.

Lou took a couple drags while he thought. "So, what do you want to do? I mean, I came strapped."

Lou nodded for Corey to walk with him to the back of his car. He looked up and down the empty road a couple of times before opening his trunk and revealing all of the artillery he'd purchased from Danny.

"Why are you riding around with all this shit?" Corey said. "This shit ain't legal, Lou. That's some rookie shit!"

"I know, big bro, my bad. But what are we gonna do about Summer? We just can't leave her in there."

Corey was already a few steps ahead of Lou; that's why he had called him. Although Corey was mad at Lou for riding around dirty like he was, he was glad the extra firepower was on deck. If he could remember correctly, the black SUV that was following Luv around all night was still at the house early this morning when Corey drove by there.

"Look, we gon' run up in there, snatch Summer, and get the hell out of there," Corey said and passed Lou one of the vests. "Stay close to me and watch my back. Smoke anybody moving with a gun in his hand."

Corey barked out instructions as he slammed a clip into one of the compact AR-15s. Corey wasn't playing any games. If something had happened to Summer, everybody in that house was going to die.

Ariana patted Summer on her face several times before saying the words, "Sheep, sheep."

Summer hesitantly opened her eyes to observe the adorable little girl sitting on the bed wearing only a Pull-Ups. All she could do was return a smile to the toddler who was grinning while munching down on her two little fingers.

"Ariana!" Luv yelled as he walked up the stairs.

Somehow, Ariana had climbed out of her high chair while he was on an important business call and she made her way up the stairs.

"She's in here!" Summer yelled then quietly apologized to the infant for telling on her.

Luv came into the room shaking his head while flashing a wide smile. "Come here, you little monster." He playfully jumped on the bed in front of Ariana and tickled her until she couldn't take it anymore. Snot, spit, and tears covered her young face, remnants of how hard she was laughing.

Summer looked on, joyful at how much fun Luv and his daughter were having.

"I'm sorry. She must have snuck away from the nanny and me," he explained.

Summer was about to let him know that it was okay, but her phone started to ring. She reached over and grabbed it off the nightstand. "I gotta take this," she told Luv after seeing that it was Corey.

He scooped Ariana up, tossed her over his shoulder, and playfully carried her out the door.

"Yeah, wassup?" Summer sat up in bed.

"Yeah, wassup?" Corey mocked her. "Why are you just now answering ya phone? Don't you know we were about to run up in that motherfucker to come get you?" Corey said as he drove by Luv's house. He and Lou were ready to move out.

"Don't do that. Just meet me at the spot in an hour. We good," Summer told him.

The truth of the matter was Summer wasn't good and she felt like she was going to have to come up with the money some other way. Nothing about the setup felt right anymore. Luv was a good son and a great father to his beautiful baby girl, who Summer had grown fond of. There was also the fact that Luv had taken her virginity. Up until last night, she had gotten eaten out before, but she had never let a man penetrate her. The way he made her body feel was amazing, and it was a feeling that she wasn't ready to say good-bye to. She wasn't going to be able to go through with it.

"One hour," she said and ended the call. Summer got out of the bed to find some clothes to put on.

Luv came back into the room after giving Ariana back to the nanny. "Why are you off so fast, beautiful? You didn't even give me a chance to make you breakfast." He watched Summer scurry around the room putting articles of clothing on as she went.

"I shouldn't be here, Luv." She looked around the area for her other shoe.

He calmly walked over to her and stopped her in her tracks. "Look at me, Spring," he instructed.

She didn't want to, but she couldn't help herself.

"Tell me what's going on," he quizzed.

Summer was tempted, but she declined to tell him. How could she inform him that she was there to rob him? That she was there to take what he'd worked hard for? Better yet, how was she going to explain to him that she was not who she thought she was? How crazy would she sound trying to explain to him that she was Spring's twin sister?

"Is it me? Did I do something wrong?"

"No, you didn't do anything wrong. Oh, God, you did everything right, and that's why I have to go," Summer answered.

He knew it was something more, Luv could tell by her body language. He didn't want her to leave without him trying to find out what it was.

"Spring, please let me help you. I don't care what it is," he said with a sincere look in his eyes. "Tell me. Just tell me," he insisted.

Summer so wanted to confide in him. Maybe he could help her. She decided to try her hand, thinking that the worst thing he could do was say no or kill her if he found out the truth of the matter.

"I need to come up with one hundred thousand dollars by today or I'm about to have a shitload of problems in my life." Summer dropped her head in submission.

She looked back up and Luv had walked away shaking his head. He went over to his walk-in closet, grabbed a box, then walked back over to the bed where Summer was. He opened the box and began to pull out stacks of money, tossing it onto the bed. He counted the money bands around the cash until it equaled up to $100,000. He then closed the box and put it on the side.

"Here's the money you needed by today," he said, pushing the money across the bed.

Summer looked from the money to Luv in confusion. "Why are you doing this?" she asked, walking over to the bed. "You still don't even know me like that."

"I just want to have breakfast in bed wit' you." He reached out his hand for her to come sit on the bed where he was.

She walked over and took a seat on the bed between his legs, submitting to his request. He was definitely a different type of breed, and to date, no one had ever treated her the way that he had over the past couple of days. Now she was really confused, but this time it was due to the way she was feeling about him.

"You know I'ma pay you every dime back." She smiled and leaned in to kiss him then pushed him back on the bed and straddled him.

Luv honestly didn't care about the money. He had plenty of it and could afford to lend a helping hand here and there. To him, Spring was worth much more than what he had.

"You want breakfast in bed, right?" Summer asked seductively, pulling her shirt over her head. Luv nodded with a sexy smile on his face. "Don't worry. I'ma give you plenty to eat."

She had a few things to take care of today, but everything was at a standstill for the moment. She wanted to relish Luv for just a little longer.

Benny, Santana, and a couple of females were in the restaurant having lunch when Detective Keys and Detective Allen walked in. One of Benny's guys stopped them at the door, knowing they were cops. The commotion caught Benny's attention, prompting him to get up from his table.

"You know we don't serve ya kind around these parts," Benny said walking up and recognizing Keys. "If y'all don't have a warrant, I think it's time for y'all to leave."

"We just need to have a word with you, Benny," Keys said. "We also have some valuable information that could be beneficial to your freedom."

Upon hearing that, Benny dismissed his boy with a wave of his hand. When it came to his freedom, he was interested in what they had to say. "Go ahead and talk."

"We know about the dope at the storage facility and how a couple of your people were murdered behind it—"

"Whoa, whoa, whoa. Do I look like a fuckin' fool? What da hell are you talking about?" Benny snapped, cutting the detective off.

"It's not you we're after. We want Spring," Detective Allen clarified.

"Yeah, this conversation is off the record and we will never use it against you," Keys promised.

Benny wasn't a snitch and this was probably the longest he'd ever conversed with the law. It was a must that he find out what info they had on him. "Look, I know some shit, but I'm not saying nothing until y'all tell me what y'all got on me," Benny stated.

Detectives Keys and Allen looked at each other. They knew that Benny couldn't be trusted, but Keys was desperate and wanted to bring Spring down pretty badly. He was willing to lose his job behind it, too.

"Look, you're being investigated by the feds. They have somebody posted up a couple of blocks away right now watching this restaurant. I don't know how much info they have on you or what evidence they've accumulated so far, but the one thing I can tell you is that you have an informant within ya circle," Keys explained.

Benny looked at the back of the restaurant where Santana and a couple of his boys were looking on. It was one thing to have the feds on his tip, but it was another thing to have a rat in his crew. For that good piece of information, Benny was going to throw Keys a bone.

"Yeah, ya girl, Spring, came in here the other day—"

Keys cut him off, knowing it was impossible that Spring could do or be anywhere since she was in the county jail. "Come on, Benny, cut the shit. Give it to me straight," Keys demanded.

"I'm being straight up with you. I know for a fact that she was in here three days ago."

Benny went on to tell him that Spring had somebody stealing from her. It was somebody in her crew. He told Keys that Spring was running dope for Mike and she had blamed Vick for stealing the drugs from her.

"Next thing I know, Vick made the news. I'm not saying she did it, but I guess you can use common sense to figure out the rest. Now, if you will excuse me, I have a few things to talk to my people about," Benny said, ending the conversation. He knew he was lying about Spring killing Vick, but he figured he might as well pin it on her if she was already facing murder charges.

Detectives Keys and Allen left the restaurant pissed, feeling that Benny had pulled the wool over their eyes. They had given up a lot of information for nothing. Keys was familiar with Vick's homicide and knew beyond a shadow of a doubt that Spring couldn't have done it. The other information Benny provided was going to be sifted through thoroughly by Keys, and what was useful he was going to use, and everything else would be discarded. If Benny thought that he had gotten over, he was wrong. His problem with the law had only just begun.

Corey paced back and forth in the hideout, frustrated with the lack of communication from Summer. She was supposed to have been there an hour ago and it was almost time for them to meet up with Gary.

"She slippin', dog. I'm telling you she ain't ready for this shit. Spring would have been here."

Just as Corey was popping off, the locks on the front door turned. Summer walked into the house and froze. All eyes were on her and she could feel the tension.

"What?" she asked like she was innocent of any wrongdoing.

"What? That's all you got to say is, 'what'? Why haven't you tried to call? You said that you would be here at twelve. It's one twenty-four!" Corey snapped. "We didn't know what was going on in that house."

Summer took her Louis Vuitton bag and dumped the money that she got from Luv out onto the coffee table. "You wanna know what was going on in that house? This is what was going down," she said, pointing to the money. "And let me make myself clear: I'm not my sister. I do shit my way, and as long as the job gets done, there shouldn't be any problems."

After all that she had been through the night before, nobody could tell her what and how to do anything.

"So, what, you think you runnin' shit now? You think you—"

"I know I'm runnin' shit, and if you don't like it then do something about it," Summer shot back. She reached into her back pocket and pulled out her gun.

Corey upped his gun as well, and that's when Lou had enough. He jumped up from the couch and stood right in the middle of them.

"Hold da fuck up. Y'all two is trippin'," Lou based, looking back and forth from Corey to Summer. "Put those fuckin' guns up. We got shit to do."

"Next time you pull a gun out on me I'ma tear ya ass out the frame. I don't give a fuck who you think you are," Corey threatened as he tucked his gun back into his waist. "Remember, you're just a fill-in."

Lou looked into Summer's eyes and could see that she wasn't going for anything. Her whole attitude and body language had changed since yesterday, and surprisingly she was starting to act just like her sister. Lou wasn't the only one who could see that Summer had bossed up.

Detective Keys sat in his car with his partner going over everything that Benny had told him. The thing that stuck out the most was when he said that Spring had stopped by his place the other day. Everything else besides that made sense, including Spring running dope for Mike.

Out of pure curiosity, Keys ran a check to see if Spring had any siblings.

"I tell you one thing, this case is all over the place," Allen said, looking out his window. "This girl is into more shit than we originally thought."

Keys was about to comment, but then his phone began to vibrate. It was Pam at the station.

"Okay, Spring Stewart has one other sibling and, get this, it's her twin and her name is Summer Stewart. According to hospital records, she was born a full two minutes after her sister," Pam explained to Detective Keys, who was shocked at the new information. Pam explained that Summer was a student at UNC.

"She has a twin sister," Keys looked over and told Allen.

"A twin sister? So that means Benny might not have been lying about Spring coming to his restaurant a couple of days ago," Allen suggested. "Do you think that's possible?'

"I don't know, but we sure gon' find out," Keys said and put the gear in drive.

It was going to take the detectives a little more than two hours to get to the college, but the lead was well worth it. Keys had more than a few questions to ask Summer and, for her sake, she'd better answer each and every one of them truthfully.

On the drive to meet up with Gary, nobody said too much of anything. Corey focused on the road, Summer gazed out of the window, and Lou sat in the back seat wondering how long the silent treatment was going to last.

"Ay, yo, you two are killing me back here. We all supposed to be family," Lou spoke out, breaking the silence.

Summer had been thinking about her actions ever since they left the hideout. She honestly could admit that she was wrong in what she did. Apologizing just wasn't her strong suit but, for the sake of the crew, she swallowed her pride.

"I'm sorry for acting like an asshole," she said, looking over at Corey. "And I'm sorry for pulling out a gun on you, too."

Corey pulled over on the side of the road and threw the car in park. "Listen, Summer, everything that we do needs to be done a certain way and at a certain time. When we go outside of the plan, shit goes wrong. Vick is a prime example, and look where he's at," Corey barked.

"I know, and from now on I promise I will listen to you and never deviate from the plan. Just don't be mad at me and please don't tell my sister."

She wasn't Spring, but looking over at her sure did remind Corey of her. For that, there was no way he could continue to be mad at her. At the same time, he needed her to know how serious things could get in the streets.

"So, are we cool?" Summer asked and play punched his arm.

For the first time that day, he cracked a smile. "Yeah, we cool now. Call that nigga and tell him that we five minutes out," he said, referring to Gary.

Summer was more than happy to follow orders.

When they pulled up to the underpass, Gary was already there, leaning against his car smoking a cigarette. He let Summer have it as soon as she got out of the car.

"If you're late like this on the day of the robbery, you can forget about the plan working. And you can also forget about getting your money back."

Corey gave him the bag with the $200,000 inside. Gary opened it and took a peek in.

"A'ight, pay close attention, 'cause deviating from this will cost you your life," Gary began.

Corey looked over at Summer to remind her that he had just told her the same thing about deviating. Gary broke the whole thing down in detail, letting everybody know what was expected out of them. He gave new details, suggesting there was going to be a little more than $4 million in the truck as soon as they pulled out of the building, so hitting them at the first drop-off spot was the best chance for them to take everything.

"So take a few days to get familiar with the route; then on Thursday we'll rendezvous for some last minute touchups," Gary said. "Any questions?"

When Summer and Corey didn't say anything, Gary tossed the bag into his back seat, got into his car, and drove off. He was vicious in playing both sides of the fence and selling the heist to both Spring and Benny. He wasn't going to do it at first, but then he thought about the extra money he could make by sending both parties on a crash course. He was already up a little over a half million dollars between the two, so whether the heist was successful by one of the two groups or if they failed, Gary was good financially and would be on the next thing smoking out of the city.

"You think we can handle this or should we get another person?" Lou asked Corey as they stood under the underpass.

Lou was a little concerned that all of what Gary told them may have been a little too much for Summer to handle. Corey had faith in Summer and knew that as long as she stayed the course she would handle her role with ease.

"Nah, we good. Now let's get out of here so we can go check the route out," Corey concluded as he, Summer, and Lou got back in the car.

Chapter 19

Luv walked out onto the balcony of his bedroom where Summer stood, looking out at the beautiful scenery. It was obvious that she had something on her mind.

"So, do you wanna talk about it?" he asked, walking up and wrapping his arms around her waist.

Summer had the heist on her mind real heavy, but she wasn't going to tell Luv that. "You know, I wonder how long this thing we have will last. I mean, I know you're going to get tired of me sooner or later."

Luv rested his chin on her shoulder with his face pressed against the side of hers. "You wanna know something crazy? I was just thinking the same thing last night while I watched you sleep. I still can't believe I bagged you in the first place." He chuckled.

Summer turned around to face him. "I gotta tell you something, but you have to give me ya word that you're gonna believe me."

"Oh, this is good." Luv smiled, curious as to what she had to say.

"No, give me ya word first," she insisted, pinching him on the side.

"A'ight, a'ight, I give you my word," he caved.

Summer cleared her throat, took in a deep breath then exhaled. "You were the first person I've ever been with," she confessed.

Luv cocked his head to the side and threw up one eyebrow. "You mean like you was a virgin?" he asked to get some clarity. "I mean, you were tight as hell, but, wow."

"Oh, my goodness, I can't believe I told you that." She blushed, planting her forehead in the center of his chest.

Luv could tell that she was embarrassed, but Luv felt honored to be the one she chose to give it away to. Being the only man who had ever gone inside of her made Luv want to be with her even more. It was rare to run into a woman like that, and for that reason alone, he was going to do his best to keep her.

"Ay." He lifted her chin up so she could look him in his eyes. "In my life, I've only made three promises. I promised my mother that I would never hit a female. I promised my third grade teacher that I was going to be rich by the time I finished high school. And I promised my child's mother right before she died that I would take care of Ariana. To date, I've kept my promises, and today I'm going to make a promise to you. I give you my word that I will be here for you as long as you want me to be, and that as long as I got you, I'm not gonna be with anybody else." As he spoke, Luv had nothing but sincerity in his eyes.

The crazy thing was that Summer believed him. She felt so guilty for lying to him. She wanted to tell him the truth, but she knew now wasn't the time. She knew she couldn't blow her cover until everything went through on Friday and things with her sister were all worked out. She thanked God that the liquor and sex had taken over last night and she hadn't blurted everything out then.

Her biggest concern was how she was going to tell him that she wasn't Spring. She wondered how he would take the news. She tried to reason and convince herself that it wasn't a big deal. It was not like she was lying about who she was. She had been herself every time they'd been together. He'd just have to accept that her name was actually Summer and she wasn't this big time player like her sister. Now, all she could think about was making it through Friday so she could get back to being herself.

She was hoping and praying that Luv would be understanding and that after she told him the truth, he'd still be true to his promise. In a perfect world, Summer would get her happy ending and reap the benefits of being rich and having a good man stand by her side.

Lou had two bad white chicks in his hotel room performing like they were starring in a porno. He had heavy weed and drink all over the place, and there was no limit as to what was going down in this room today. Friday was a big day, and although the plan was set, and they had an inside man, the possibility of something going wrong was still alive. If these were going to be his last days in the streets, or even on this earth, Lou wanted to be sure that he did it big before he went out. He wanted to have fun, chill with the family, and make plans in the event he did get away with the heist.

There was so much Lou could do with a million dollars and, if given the opportunity, he was going to make the best of it. Until that time came, he was going to live in the moment, which meant treating himself with the pleasures life had to offer.

"Can you see if Gary will let us delay it a week?" Spring asked Corey as they sat in the visiting room. The court date for Spring's bail hearing had been moved up to the coming Friday, which, unfortunately, happened to be the same day as the heist. The chances of Gary changing the date or delaying it any further were slim to none. None being the strongest possible outcome.

"Spring, I have everything under control," Corey assured her, knowing that she was mainly concerned about Summer. She knew Summer hadn't done anything of that magnitude in her life, so Spring's concerns were well placed.

"I just don't want anything to happen to her, you know?" Spring spoke up.

"Look at me. Do you think I'm about to let something happen to your sister? You should know me better than that by now," Corey replied. "Besides, ya sista is crazy as hell." He chuckled, thinking about Summer pulling a gun out on him. "If I didn't think that she could handle herself, she wouldn't be doing it."

If Spring trusted anyone with her sister's life, it was Corey. The love he had for Spring was more than enough evidence to prove that Summer was going to be safe.

"That's one of the reasons why I love you," Spring said, catching Corey off guard.

That was the first time he'd heard those words come out of her mouth, and just to be sure he'd heard those words right, he asked her to repeat what she'd said.

"I said, that's one of the reasons why I love you." Spring leaned out of her seat to give him a kiss. She kissed him so hard the guard had to call out her name to break it up. "I know I should have told you this a long time ago, but with everything going on, I never had the chance. But I promise that as soon as I get home I'm going to prove it to you."

To hear her say those words meant a lot to Corey. He was so shocked, he just nodded his head. One thing for sure, he couldn't wait for her to come home and honor her promise.

Ever since Detective Keys had told Benny about the feds watching him, he was more precise with what he did, where he went, and what came out of his mouth. Though he wasn't able to pinpoint the rat in his camp, he kept his drug business moving, but his involvement with it was limited. He personally wasn't going to be making any drops or picking up any money, nor was he having any more conversations about anything illegal in the restaurant.

"So what about the other thing?" Santana asked as he and Benny stood in the back alleyway of the restaurant. He was referring to the heist and whether he still had the green light on it.

"I paid that muthafucka three hundred thousand for that sting. You better believe we're going through with it. Besides, the feds are watching me, so you should be able to slip away and get the job done without them knowing," Benny said.

The dope was going to be hard to move, so the heist was the next big thing and would provide enough money for Benny to go on the run for a while. He made those plans the moment he got word about the feds. If he could be on the run for at least five years without being involved in any criminal activities, the statute of limitations would eat the case up, and the feds would have to start from scratch. So, Benny needed this heist to go down nice and smooth. His freedom was riding on its success.

"And what about Spring?" Santana asked, trying to make sure all their T's were crossed and their I's were dotted.

"Fuck Spring. I don't care what happens. She better have my money."

Benny didn't have any picks when it came to his greed, especially now when he really needed the money. It might've seemed right in his eyes, but ultimately it was going to come back and bite him in the ass.

***

Around five o'clock in the morning, Summer attempted to sneak out of bed without waking Luv. She wanted to hurry up, get dressed, and be out the door so she could meet up with Corey and Lou. Today was Friday and it was go time. Summer was more nervous than she'd ever been, but she was focused on the task at hand. She'd been up since four in the morning just thinking about everything. Her emotions were everywhere. A part of her was wondering if this would be the last time she lay next to Luv. She was having doubts about whether she should still tell him the truth about who she was tonight after the heist. She was debating whether she should tell him now, in case she didn't make it.

"Where are you going this early?" Luv interrupted her thoughts. "It's like five in the morning." His voice sounded groggy, having just woken up.

"I know. I gotta go take care of something important," she answered as she put on her clothes.

Luv didn't know anything about the heist, and Summer wanted to keep it that way. She could hear him now, explaining how she didn't have to do it and how he would take care of her.

"I should be free this afternoon, but I'll call you if something else comes up," Summer told him.

Luv became a little concerned. He sat up in the bed, turned the lamp light on, and wiped his eyes. "Are you okay, Spring?" he asked.

Summer quickly put her sneakers on so she could hurry up and get out of there before the round of questioning began.

"Yeah, I'm good. It's nothing that serious," she replied and crawled back onto the bed to give him a kiss goodbye.

She wanted to tell him something in case this was their last time together, but she couldn't bring herself to say it.

It was way too early to be talking about love, even though in her heart she did feel like she had love for him. She didn't want to mess things up or make things complicated with those words. Keeping it simple was the best route to take.

"Plan a special date for us tonight," Summer said. She kissed him one more time before leaving.

Luv had a gut feeling that something wasn't right, but there wasn't much he could do except hope that whatever she did have going on worked in her favor. He would hate to lose her this early in the game. All he could do was try to shake that strange feeling and plan their date for later on tonight.

6:00 a.m.

Santana, Carlos, and Rico sat in the basement of the restaurant loading up their weapons and going over the plan. Santana wanted to make sure everyone knew what positions they were playing and what route would be taken after they got the money.

"There's no room for error, so if you fuck up out there, you're on ya own," Santana warned.

Rico and Carlos sat there listening, all the while wiping down the guns to get rid of any DNA or fingerprints. Messing around in an armored truck heist, somebody was bound to be shot.

"This shit ain't no game, *papi,* and if any of those guards get stupid, don't hesitate to put a bullet in his head."

He really didn't have to tell that to Rico and Carlos because when it came to gunplay, that's all they did. Problem children were what the people in the neighborhood knew them to be, and that was from the age of eleven. As far as popping that pistol, they were about their business.

"A'ight y'all, go home, kiss ya wife and kids, and be back here in an hour," Santana told them. Santana himself had to jump on the phone and make a quick call to his girlfriend, just in case he didn't make it back.

Today, things were about to get real and nobody was safe, nor were there any guarantees. It was ugly, but it was a part of the game that Santana knew all too well.

7:00 a.m.

Gary stood at his locker changing into his uniform when out of nowhere his phone began to ring. Kelsey's face popped up on the screen and, for a minute, he wasn't going to answer it. He was different from most, and really didn't want to hear the voice of the person he loved more than anything right before he was about to commit a crime.

"Hey, baby, it's busy today," Gary answered, trying to make the call brief.

"I know, baby. You just got up and left without saying anything. You know I have a shitty day when I don't get my morning kiss," she semi-whined.

"I'm sorry. You know I love you. Here, mwuah!" he said, blowing her a big kiss. Kelsey blew him one back. "A'ight, baby, let me get back to work. We'll go out for dinner when I get home."

Kelsey told Gary that she loved him one last time before hanging up the phone. He had to let her words roll off his shoulders, knowing what they'd do to him if he took them in. He definitely wouldn't be able to go through with the heist if all he thought about was how it would affect her if things went south.

"G-money!" Tony yelled when he came into the locker room.

Gary's other partner, Jake, came right in behind him, throwing a couple of play punches to Gary. "You ready for today?" Jake asked, holding his hand up for the special handshake they gave each other every day.

The three of them were pretty tight after rolling in the same armored truck for the past year. Gary felt horrible for putting them in harm's way, but that was something he was willing to deal with.

"A'ight, y'all, you know what time it is," Tony said, huddling the boys up for their daily prayer. "God keep us safe and sharp while riding around with the devil's food. Please allow this money to be used for something good and not evil. Amen."

Gary finished getting dressed then headed up to control to sign out the money he was supposed to be delivering today. This was going to be a long and tough day, and Gary made a little sidebar prayer asking God to forgive him for the sins that he was about to commit. He was going to need it, along with a few blessings as well.

8:00 a.m.

Spring was shackled with the rest of the females in a holding cell waiting to be transferred to the courthouse. She couldn't help but to think about her crew and how they were en route right now to take care of some major business. Just the thought of it had her palms sweating. The adrenaline rush for doing a job like this would be off the charts, something Spring chased on a daily basis out there on the streets. She only wished that she could have been there to execute the plan.

"Stewart, Crosby, Jenkins, and Ford, please step forward and line up against the wall!" the correctional officer yelled.

Spring felt like cattle the way that she and the other females were being handled. It wasn't just the females, but also the male inmates who were being treated like crap.

"This shit ain't nothin' but modern-day slavery," the female who was standing in front of Spring said.

Spring had to agree. Out of the twenty-four people who were going to court that day, at least twenty of them were black. This whole jail experience had left the worst taste in Spring's mouth and, at this point, all she wanted to do was get out of there and move on with her life. She had even thought of going legal after one major score. Only time would tell if those thoughts manifested into something truthful. If things went as well as expected today, she just might have a shot at making those thoughts a reality.

Chapter 20

9:00 a.m. (Go Time)

Summer, Corey, and Lou drove back to back in two stolen cars toward the Richmond shopping complex. There were a number of stores there, but PNC Bank was the target. It sat off in the corner of the shopping center by itself. They pulled up and parked in the bank's parking lot, but stayed in their vehicles until Corey gave the green light from the van he was sitting in by himself.

"You good?" Lou asked Summer, who looked a little nervous behind the wheel. Her palms were sweating like crazy in her latex gloves.

"Yeah, I'm good. I just wanna get this shit over with," she answered, looking around the shopping center for any unwanted cops.

"Just be cool, take in a couple of deep breaths, and think about taking a vacation to Barbados next month," Lou told her, trying to get her to calm down.

She took a deep breath and was cool until the knock at her front window scared the life out of her. It was Corey, telling her and Lou to get out of the car.

"Yo, it's time to rock and roll," Corey said, looking down at his watch.

Not giving them a chance to change their minds, he stormed through the parking lot heading right for the bank. Lou and Summer were right behind him, guns in hand, down by their side. This was the moment of truth, and what Summer had been waiting for all morning. Her heart had dropped to the pit of her stomach and, by the time she looked up, Corey was pulling the mask down over his face and walking through the front doors of the bank. Lou's mask went down too, and as she got up to the door, Summer's mask came down as well.

"Everybody get ya fuckin' hands in the air."

Benny looked into his rearview mirror and could see that the federal agents who were watching his restaurant had begun to pursue him. That's exactly what he wanted them to do, taking the attention off of Santana long enough for him to slip away. The plan had worked perfectly. Santana, Rico, and Carlos were on the move, free from the watchful eye of the feds.

"Go and get that money," Benny mumbled to himself as he maneuvered through traffic. His job was to keep the feds busy all day, which he enjoyed.

"A'ight, gentlemen, we're at the first stop of the day!" Tony yelled out to Gary and Jake, who were in the back of the truck with the money.

Tony turned into the shopping complex and pulled right up to the front of the bank. He looked around for any suspicious movement, and once he deemed it to be clear, he tapped on the cabin to give Gary and Jake the okay.

"A'ight, bags two and six," Jake said, reading from the chart. Gary grabbed both of them and unlocked the back door.

"Man, after y'all have this baby, a lot of stress is gonna be lifted off your shoulders," Jake said, getting back to the conversation they were having.

Gary carried the bags while Jake kept a sharp eye out for any trouble. Once they got up to the bank's door, he relaxed a little. From that moment on, everything happened in a flash.

"Hands up! Hands up!" Corey yelled as he came from behind the partition by the door.

Jake thought back to his training and swiftly reached for his weapon, but Lou was all over him, coming across the floor with his gun pointed directly at Jake's face.

"Okay, okay," Jake submitted, holding his hands in the air while kneeling on the ground.

Gary dropped the bags and lay down on the ground, interlocking his hands behind his back as he was instructed by Corey.

Summer stayed behind the tellers' booth, holding employees and a few customers on the ground at gunpoint. Gary and Jake were disarmed, and only Jake was put in zip ties.

Corey explained to Gary what was going to happen next, loud enough so Jake could hear what was going on. For effect, Corey hit Gary over his head with the butt of the gun. Lou had scooped up the money bags and was waiting for Summer to get the cash back to the car.

"If you move, you die," Summer threatened, pointing her gun at the people lying on the floor.

You couldn't pay any of them to lift their heads up. She walked over to Lou, switched the money into another bag then headed for the door. Her mask was removed before she exited the building, so Tony didn't pay her any mind. He sat in the armored truck texting his daughter, unaware of what was going on.

Only when he glanced over and saw Gary walking toward the truck with a masked gunman walking behind him did Tony realize that it was a robbery. He started to grab the radio and call it in, but out of nowhere a man with a lit Molotov cocktail threw the bottle full of gasoline right at the nose of the truck, engulfing the front in flames.

The huge fireball caught Corey off guard, and when he looked over, two men were running through the bank's parking lot coming straight for him. Summer, who was standing by the stolen car, peeped the blitz and automatically drew the baby Desert Eagle from her side. She started firing rounds at the two gunmen. She also fired rounds at Tony, who was getting out of the truck with his weapon drawn.

"Open it!" Corey demanded, pushing Gary against the back door.

The two unknown gunmen fired back at Summer, forcing her to take cover behind the car. Lou looked on from the bank and waited for the right moment to come out gunning.

Pop! Pop! Pop! Pop!

Lou hit one of the gunmen in the back twice and the other in his arm. The whole scene was chaotic. Bullets were flying all over the place.

Tony made his way around to the back of the truck and hesitated at the door. When he looked in, he saw Gary and Corey working together to round up the rest of the money.

Gary's and Tony's eyes met, and before Gary could say or do anything, the same guy who threw the Molotov cocktail walked up behind him, jammed his gun into Tony's back, and fired twice.

Corey opened fire on the gunman. One of the bullets hit him in his chest, knocking him on his ass.

The gunman, determined to kill Corey, reached up and fired several shots into the cabin. The gunman attempted to get up, only having been shot in his bulletproof vest. He tried his best to get off a better shot. He had Corey in his crosshairs, and right when he was about to pull the trigger, Summer walked up behind him and put a bullet in the back of his head.

"We gotta go!" Summer yelled, hearing police sirens getting closer.

On cue, Lou pulled up to the side of the burning truck in the stolen car. Corey wasted no time loading the rest of the money into the car. He knew that he didn't have much time, but he had to know who had just tried to kill him. He pulled the mask off, and after getting a good look at his face, Corey jumped in the car and sped off.

The scene they left behind was horrific. It was something only seen in the movies. Two dead, a burning armored truck, and a bank full of customers. They left right in the nick of time, too, because police were right on the scene less than a minute after they pulled off.

"Who da fuck was that?" Summer asked frantically as they switched cars.

Corey was more focused on loading up the money right then. He already knew who it was and he was going to make it his business to holler at the man who sent them as soon as possible. The task at hand was to put as much distance as possible between them and the bank. At this point, they weren't out of hot water just yet. Cop cars were everywhere, along with helicopters in the sky, all of whom were looking for the black Ford Taurus that had fled from the scene. Plenty of work needed to be done to ensure the success of this heist.

Spring sat in the courtroom talking to her lawyer before the judge appeared on the bench. He was going over the terms of bail that the DA had requested. The government wanted Spring to be on house arrest until the conclusion of the case. Restrictions were made on leaving the state and a urinalysis twice a week to make sure she wasn't using any type of drugs.

"Of course, I'll be objecting to these terms," McMan said, pulling his glasses down. "Now this judge got a hard on for you, so I don't think he's going to make it easy for you to go free. Expect a high bail. I'm more—"

"All rise," the bailiff announced, coming into the courtroom.

The judge came out and took a seat on the bench. The man looked so mean, Spring thought that she wasn't going to get any rhythm. The DA went right to work, explaining all the reasons why Spring shouldn't get a bail. She stated that Spring was a menace to society, having been caught twice in twenty-four hours with a gun. The DA didn't even address the terms of bail. She was shooting for it to be denied all the way around the board first.

McMan let her talk for over ten minutes without saying anything, and as soon as it was his turn he blasted the government and didn't hold back. He explained how his client was being treated too harshly, and how they were only going off a hunch that Spring had been involved in a homicide. To date, no charges had been filed in accordance with those allegations, nor was the investigation still active. McMan stated that to deny Spring a bail would be a miscarriage of justice.

The judge ate it up, but he wasn't about to let Spring bail out so easily. At the end of the hearing and after considering both sides, he made his ruling. He ordered that the bail be set at one hundred thousand and that she remain on house arrest until the conclusion of the case. He was really trying to crush Spring by making the bail so high. He didn't think that she would be able to make it, but he was in for a shock. The only thing Spring was worried about was the house arrest. She wasn't going to be able to move around like she wanted to. But if that was the only way that she was going to be released, then she surely was going to take it in stride.

***

The whole shopping center was full of cop cars and FBI agents combing the place for evidence. Special Agent Kelley took the lead on the investigation, and from the moment he showed up on the scene he had been working.

"You can let forensics in!" Agent Kelley yelled, waving in the unit.

His partner, Special Agent David Knox, was also heading the investigation and making progress. "We got a switch car about two miles east of here," Knox walked up and told Kelley. "I'm on my way over there. Are you staying?"

"Yeah, I'm staying here. I don't want anybody fuckin' up my crime scene," Kelley responded.

A veteran of the force for ten years, eight years of his time on the force had been spent investigating bank robberies. He specialized in it, and on one or two occasions he had investigated an armored truck heist. Today, he was having the best of both worlds. An armored truck heist at a bank. This was the type of case where Kelley knew that sleep wasn't going to come easy. The only thing about it was he was up for the job and so was his partner.

"Nooooo," Corey yelled, smacking a bag full of newspaper off the table. "He played us. That muthafucka played us!" he said through clenched teeth.

Out of five bags that came from the armored truck, only two of them had money in them, equaling up to about $650,000.

"Why would he play us like this?" Summer asked, picking up some of the newspaper and throwing it back onto the table.

"It was a setup. The muthafucka was trying to play the fifty," Corey answered, thinking about the face he saw under the mask.

Summer tried to say something, but Corey shushed her as he went into deep thought. He knew the game all too well and came up with Gary's plot in his head. Corey put two and two together in seconds.

"What are you thinking about, man?" Lou asked, disliking the silence in the room.

"Just like I said. Gary set us up. Vick must've told Benny about the heist before he died, and the only way Benny could have gotten the specifics of the job was if he paid Gary himself." It all came together in his mind.

"How do you know all of this? What makes you think that it was Benny?" Summer asked.

"The muthafucka you shot in the back of his head was one of Benny's boys. I remember him from the night at the restaurant. He had the same tattoo of the city's skyline on his neck. I knew it was him."

Everybody let out a frustrated sigh as the information sank in. Summer had her mind made up and was ready to go and deal with the issue. There was no other way to handle the situation with Benny except for what she knew he'd respect, which was gunplay. One thing for sure and two things for certain, Benny's actions had consequences, and with all the high tempers in the room, things were about to get extremely ugly.

Gary cracked his eyes open and knew immediately that he was in the hospital. The feeling of something missing from inside of him was obvious. The bullet that went through his vest had done severe damage to his stomach, ultimately causing the doctors to remove his spleen. A second bullet knocked a chunk of flesh out of the top of his shoulder, but the injury was minor compared to the gut shot.

"Hey. Hey, can you hear me?" a voice asked.

Gary could hear somebody snapping their fingers in front of his face, but his vision was too blurred to see anything yet. It took a couple of minutes, but eventually Gary's eyes adjusted well enough for him to see a tall white well-dressed man standing over him chewing gum.

"My name is Agent Kelley. What happened?"

Gary's throat was dry and he could barely talk. "We got robbed," he managed to say. His eyes were starting to get heavy and Kelley knew that he didn't have much time before he went under again.

"Did you see any of their faces?" Kelley asked.

Gary's eyes closed and it didn't look like they were going to open back up anytime soon.

With the anesthesia still in his system, along with the pain medication taking effect, Gary wasn't going to be able to answer any questions in the near future. The doctor came in the room and explained to Kelley that he would have better luck the next day. Kelley wanted answers as to what went down, and although Jake had given him a full account of what he witnessed through the whole ordeal, it didn't explain all that had taken place outside.

Right now, Gary was the only person who could bring some clarity with regard to that portion of the robbery. Agent Kelley had plenty of patience and was going to be back first thing in the morning, bright-eyed and bushy-tailed.

Spring got back to the block around five o'clock in the evening and wasted no time jumping on the phone. The bail was sky high, but she knew that it would be paid, especially after what had gone down today.

"Damn, what da hell!" she said in frustration after Summer's phone went to voicemail.

She tried again but got the same results, prompting her to try Corey's phone. There was no answer there, and when she tried to call Lou's phone, his was off too. Spring wanted to slam the receiver up against the wall. Her freedom was a mere $100,000 away. Spring tried all three of their phones again, and this time she did slam the receiver against the wall when no one answered. She was mad as hell, storming back to her cell.

Right when she got to the door of her cell, she glanced over and saw the rec room jam-packed, huddled around the TV. Karan, who was standing in the front, waved Spring over.

At first, Spring didn't feel like being bothered, but she remembered that the news was on and if the heist did go down it would be the top story.

"Girl, these muthafuckas is crazy out there," Karan said when Spring entered the room.

Sure enough, the armored truck heist was the breaking news. On the TV screen was a helicopter hovering over the scene and all that could be seen was the armored truck sitting in front of the bank burned to a crisp. Red and blue lights flashed all over the shopping center.

"So far, no suspects have been arrested," the anchor reported from the scene. "Federal agents are questioning the bank employees, along with interviewing the surviving armored truck drivers, trying to get an understanding of the brazen daytime robbery that took the life of a respected armored truck driver and severely wounded another. Two of the suspected robbers were also pronounced dead at the scene. The names of the two men have yet to be released. We'll keep you updated throughout the evening on this top story."

As the females filed out of the rec room, Spring stood there staring up at the TV with a blank look on her face. She couldn't believe what the anchor had said about the two male suspects who were dead at the scene. She just knew that it had to be Lou and Corey. The weight of it brought Spring to her knees right there on the spot. She tried to hold back her tears, but she couldn't. Losing those two was a devastating blow, one that would be hard for her to recover from.

Gary woke up again, but that time he didn't want to open his eyes. He feared that Agent Kelley would still be in the room, ready to ask a bunch of questions. Though he already had his story straight, Gary was still a little nervous now that people had been killed during the heist. Dead bodies were the recipe for a long and hard investigation, one where anything was liable to happen. All Gary could think about at this point was getting the money he had stashed away, getting Kelsey, and shooting out to Arizona. He'd rather cooperate with the authorities from a distance and at a minimum.

He wished that he had enough strength to get up and sneak out of the hospital tonight, but the chances of that were slim. He was in too much pain and there were two police officers standing right outside his door. The best thing he could do was get some rest and think about how he was going to answer the many questions that were coming his way first thing in the morning.

"Damn, I didn't even know that muthafucka got shot," Corey said as he watched the news on the television.

The city was still crawling with cops so Corey made the call that no one was to go outside nor talk on their phones, at least until things cooled down a bit.

"Yo, you think he'll hold it together?" Lou asked about Gary.

Corey thought about it and then concluded that he wasn't sure of the answer to that question. Gary talked like he was a G, but in Corey's experience, he saw some of the realest niggas fold when it came down to the feds.

"Shit," Corey blurted out, getting Lou's and Summer's attention. He jumped up from the couch in somewhat of a panic and began to pace. "Yo, we can't stay in the city. We gotta get out of here," he said, rubbing the top of his head. "We got enough money to fall back for a couple of weeks, and I think we should do that."

Summer was against that idea. She wanted to stay, bail her sister out of jail, then go and deal with Benny.

"Yo, I know this might not be the right time to put this out there, but I know a way for us to make enough money so that we all can retire," Lou interrupted.

"Come on, Lou, not right now," Corey shot back.

"Nah, let's hear what he has to say, 'cause we definitely need some more money, especially if we're talking about laying low," Summer cut in.

Lou ran upstairs to his room then came back downstairs with the letter from Trey in his hand. He passed it to Corey and told him to read it. The room was silent as Corey began to read. He read it from beginning to the end, twice, making sure he read right. The numbers made him sit down, thinking about all the things he could do with that type of money.

"What does it say?" Summer asked, breaking the silence.

Corey couldn't even explain. He had to let Summer read it herself. She too was astounded at the crazy dollar amount Trey was talking about. It made her take a seat on the couch as well.

"I know we have a lot going on right now, but as I see it, this is our way out. We'll never have to take again in our lives. We can live anywhere and do whatever we want after this one. This was the plan that my pops had for him, you, and Spring," Lou said, looking at Corey.

It was the end game. Corey vividly remembered having a similar conversation with Trey about a week before he was killed. Everything they were doing was leading up to one last score. It was the one that was supposed to retire the whole crew.

"I'm wit' it," Corey stood up and told Lou.

Summer was finishing up the last of the letter, as she too had to read it two times. When she was done, she didn't have to think about her decision.

"I'm in," she said, passing the letter back to Lou.

Despite everything that was going on, the crew was going to do what they did best, which was take. But before they did anything, Summer had something heavy on her mind. Benny and Gary were at the top of her to-do list, and she wasn't going to feel comfortable taking on this new job with them lingering around. She was also thinking about Luv. She was supposed to tell him the truth tonight, but she knew there was too much going on for her to try to contact him now.

Real love will wait for me, she thought.

"Let's tie up all the loose ends and get back to work," Summer said, grabbing the money off the coffee table and tossing it into the book bag. "First, though, we have to get Spring."

TO BE CONTINUED

Also Available
in December 2016

Carl Weber's Kingpins:

Charlotte

by

Blake Karrington

Chapter 1

Strap bobbed his head to the new Yo Gotti CD as he drove through the familiar neighborhood. He was so ready to get to the last trap house for the night and then call King so they could hit the city hard. It was Friday, and definitely a payday, but Uncle Sam wouldn't be getting a damn dime of their money. He pulled his Audi SUV in front of the dope spot with 345 on the mailbox and parked by the curb. Strap scanned the street before getting out. He may have been feeling good but not good enough to get caught slipping by some bitch-ass niggas. Strap always remembered what his granddaddy used to tell him and his cousins.

"Let your guard down, and end up six feet in the ground, little niggas."

His grandfather was a real OG and ruthless as hell. The old man was in his sixties, but niggas in the hood were still scared of his ass. As Strap walked towards the drug house, the hairs on his arm stood up. Everything looked normal around the residence, but something felt off. He waited until he got by the big oak tree in the front yard and checked his gun. The only lights he could see in the house were on the side where the kitchen was located. He looked around again. There were no unfamiliar cars on the street, but he knew that didn't mean shit.

Gripping his Colt, he slowly walked up the walkway to the front steps of the house. As he reached the top step, he heard the stone gravel behind him crunch.

Strap felt an immediate chill go down his spine as he turned. A blue flash of light and a loud sound cut through the quiet of the night. Something stung his stomach and lower back, and then, he felt a burning sensation travel down his legs.

"Fuck!" Strap yelled as he fell back against the porch.

He scanned the street, but he couldn't see who had fired the shot. His phone vibrated in his pocket, and King's name flashed across the screen when he pulled it out. He hit ACCEPT, and as he looked back up, he noticed a tall, light-skinned nigga strolling up the sidewalk. Strap tried to pop off a shot, but his hand had suddenly stopped functioning. His gun and the phone fell from his grip.

"Hey, nigga, just relax and get ready to go to sleep. Night night!" the man said as he pointed the gun at Strap and pulled the trigger. The man's laughter echoed in Strap's head as his face faded into darkness.

The Queen City, known to visitors and the rest of the world as Charlotte, North Carolina, was named after Queen Charlotte of Great Britain. *The old bird would shit bricks if she knew that a black King was driving down the streets of the city named after her, and feeling this good*, King thought as he drove his new white Jaguar XJL through the center of his hometown. Usually, he would be checking his rear view and side mirrors for the fucking cops or some bitch-ass niggas that had beef with him or his crew. But tonight, he was riding on the high of it being Friday. Nothing but a good time was ahead. With the top down, the air caressed his freshly shaved face. He had just gotten the VIP late-night treatment from his barber, Don. It was after hours, and Don didn't do shit for anyone unless they made it worth his while. Dropping a c-note to ole boy had definitely made it worth it.

King checked his reflection in the mirror and smiled. His thin mustache was lined up perfectly, and his fade was cut very low. King's thick eyebrows highlighted his light brown eyes and long eyelashes. Genetics were a great thing; even when he was young, people would always compliment him on his looks. The summer after he turned thirteen, he'd had a huge growth spurt. He had shot up six inches, and his shoulders had broadened. He now stood six feet two with caramel skin and a sculpted body that turned the heads of women and girls.

Tonight, he was feeling himself. Usually, he was on ready-set-go, but, for a brief moment, he was going to allow himself to chill. He stopped at a red light, and a group of college girls walked by. They slowed down and seductively waved at King. He nodded at them and flashed his 1000-watt smile as they smiled back. The light turned green, and he hit the accelerator. Resting his right hand on his steering wheel, he allowed his left hand to hang over the door. As he cruised, his mind drifted back to his teenage years, when he was just 16 years old.

King was in the driver's seat of his father's Mercedes. They were listening to Frankie Beverly & Maze's "Before I Let Go," which was his father's favorite song. King bobbed his head to the music while his father ran down some facts about the family business of hustling. Reggie reached over and turned down the volume on the radio.

"Listen, Ronnie," Reggie said, calling King by his first name while looking out of the passenger window. "Son, this life we in is like no other. These streets ain't got no love for no damn body. Games are for chumps, not for this business. This is some serious shit, and you can

never underestimate a man's intentions when it comes to being on top. You feel me?"

King smiled as Reggie's face began to fade into the side glass of the downtown building. His heart ached as the pain of losing his father at such a young age began to resurface. King took a deep breath. As he exhaled, his current world came back into view. As his mind cleared of his father, he pressed the VOLUME button on the radio. JAY Z's "Heart of the City (Ain't No Love)" pumped through the Bose speakers. *Damn, Dad kept it all the way real*, King thought to himself.

He approached the top of the hill and dropped the car down into second gear. This was the perfect place to test out the power of his new toy. He looked at the clock. He had spent enough time bullshitting around. He was only about twenty minutes from his trap house. He needed to meet Strap, collect his money, and make sure those fools had everything bagged up. This was not the night to be running late. It was Friday, and the spot would have been booming all day with business. He didn't like to leave a lot of cash in the hood. It would tempt folks too much.

King took out his cell phone and called his boy, Strap, to make sure everything was ready for him to pick up. The phone rang several times before the voice mail came on. King dialed Strap's number again. It rang twice this time; then, there was silence on the line.

"Hey, yo, Strap. What up, fam?" King spoke as he turned down Milton Road. The silence erupted into loud popping sounds.

"Strap? Hey, Strap, what the fuck is going on? Strap!" King yelled into his Bluetooth. He heard several more shots, and then, the line clicked. "Strap, Strap!"

King hurriedly pulled over in front of the old Circle K and jumped out. He was only a couple of blocks away from the dope house, and he needed to get his gun out of the trunk. The biggest gang in the city, CMPD, was out heavy on the streets, so he knew he needed to ride somewhat clean, especially on a Friday. King wasn't sure what he was about to walk into, but he knew he'd heard some heavy gunfire when he called Strap.

He placed the glock in the back of his pants and jumped back in the car. Quickly, he popped it into gear and sped out towards the trap house. He killed his lights as he turned down Milton. The street was quiet as King slowly approached the house. He stopped two houses down from his destination, parked near some bushes that partially hid his car, and raised his top. The streetlights were shot out as usual; the power company had stopped replacing them. King double-checked his clip and quietly made his way up to the trap house. As he approached, he could see someone slumped on the front steps. He ran over to the body and saw his man holding his stomach and moaning.

"Ah fuck, Strap! Shit," King said, kneeling beside him. "Damn, brah, where you hit?' King asked while Strap coughed and tried to pull himself up. "Nah man, stay still. Who the fuck did this?" King said, holding his friend.

King heard a gurgling sound come from Strap as he took a deep breath. He placed his ear close to Strap's lips.

Strap took another breath. As he exhaled, he whispered a name to King. "R-Red." After uttering the name, his head dropped to the left.

"Shit! Strap, come on, man. You going to be aight. Stay with me, brah," King said. He shook his friend, but the light had left his eyes.

King wanted to scream, but he knew he needed to get inside to survey the full damage. He closed Strap's eyes and stood. The screen door screeched as he opened it and walked inside the house. King kept his gun raised as he rounded the corner of the room. As he approached the kitchen, he could smell death in the air. Chris, Lil T, and Monster lay on the old cracked floor with bullets in the back of their heads and blood pooling around them.

"Fuck . . . Fuck!" King yelled as he scanned the room for any sign of his money or drugs. Nothing was there. All of it was gone.

In that moment, he didn't care about the money as his eyes fell on his fallen friends. He whispered a prayer to the God of his grandmother for their souls—the prayer of the thugs.

King stood and backed out of the kitchen. He left the house. He paused as the body of one of his closest friends lay on the steps. He hated to just leave him there like that, but he knew there was nothing else he could do for his man except make sure the people who took his life lost theirs.

"Brah, I got you. Them niggas gonna pay for this shit!" King said before jumping down the steps.

He sprinted back to the bushes and jumped in his car. He made a U-turn and headed back up Milton. As he drove up the street, he checked his rear view for any potential assailants or witnesses who may have been lurking. He was sure that the cops were only minutes away, and as he turned onto Plaza road, he heard their sirens. Shifting gears as he made his way to Harris Boulevard, he felt his blood boil as he thought about Strap and his other homeboys. His heartbeat rang in his ears. He needed to get to somewhere quick so he could process everything, and he needed someone he could trust. His family was what he needed.

King headed towards his mother and stepfather's house. There, he would find sanctuary to piece together his thoughts and figure out what he should do next.

Chapter 2

Carlton, King's stepfather, had stepped up when his biological father passed away from a heart attack. King was eighteen when his father passed. That was nearly seven years ago and Carlton had been right there for him and his mother ever since. Carlton was his father's best friend, and in many ways, he was just like King's daddy. They both were old-school street dudes who knew the game and played it well. King had never seen either of them without a custom suit, a tie, and a starched shirt. King and Carlton were as close as two people who shared the same DNA.

As he pulled up to his parents' home, he checked the time. It was late, and King had a second thought about going inside. He didn't want to wake them up, but he knew that Carlton would be upset if he wasn't told about the robbery. Using his key, he let himself into the quiet house. He could tell that his mother had decorated, yet again. The living room that once had a country theme now had earth tone covers and African art on the walls, with little elephant, lion and monkey figurines placed around the room. Hearing the TV, King shook his head and made his way downstairs to the basement.

Carlton was sitting in his favorite recliner watching an episode of Law and Order. "Hey, Son!" Carlton said, putting the TV on mute.

King gave him a weak smile as he sat down. He could see the butt of Carlton's Smith and Wesson on the side of the chair, and he was sure there was more firepower all around the room. The smile was short, and the anxiety of the evening returned.

Carlton took a sip of his Hennessey and slid to the end of the chair. "What's going on, son? Talk to me."

King looked up at him and dropped his head back down. "They dead. All of them . . . dead," King stated, fighting back tears. He ran his hands over his face and laid back on the couch. As soon as he closed his eyes, he felt sick to his stomach when Strap's lifeless stare entered his mind again.

"Who dead?" Carlton asked as he stood up.

"All my boys at the trap house—Strap, Lil T, Chris, and Monster. They murked all of them and took the money and dope. Shit, Strap died in my damn arms. I know my nigga got a couple of shots off, for sure. Before he died, he told me this nigga name Red did it."

Carlton could see the hurt in King's eyes, and the fury. He sighed and sat back down in his recliner, shaking his head as he sipped his Hen.

King stood and walked over to the bar. He grabbed a glass and poured himself a drink. After swirling it around for a moment, he sipped it. Both men were quietly trying to process everything that had gone down.

"I'm going to get them niggas, though, and I'm going to start with Red's ass. They going to get dealt with real soon!" King screamed.

"Son," Carlton responded while lighting one of his cigars, "in our business, murder brings attention we don't want or need. Murder results in bodies, and bodies result in investigation by the cops. I know you ready to wage war, but we gotta let this cool for a minute. You gotta be smart about your moves, and check your damn emotions. Keep it in your mind, but don't act too soon. I know you want vengeance right now, but let's just wait," Carlton said, blowing circles of smoke in the air.

King shook his head and allowed the Hennessey to flow down his throat as he listened to his stepfather. "Yeah, let them rest easy for now. But believe me, I am going to have Red and his crew crying like little bitches when I'm done with them."

"Such language," a soft voice said from the stairs.

King managed to flash a smile at the beautiful woman that emerged from the stairwell. His mother wore a long silk robe with the belt tied tightly around her small waist, which accentuated her hips. The gold and diamond cross that she wore around her neck touched the heart shaped tattoo she had on her chest with "Reggie," the name of King's father, inside of it.

Yolanda, or Yogi, as everyone called her, was in her late forties but had the body of a nineteen year old. Her caramel skin was near perfect. She had large brown eyes, full lips, high hips, and long relaxed hair that flowed down her back. Yolanda was a natural beauty and a true southern lady. She was soft spoken, elegant, and graceful. She could enter a room without saying a word, and heads would turn. At least that was the Yolanda side of her. Yogi was the complete opposite. She was street-educated. She would always let you know just what she felt, and was ready to whoop some ass if anyone disagreed with what she was saying. King was her only child, and she had vowed to make sure he had everything he could ever want. She would do anything to make that happen.

Yogi smiled at them both and stretched her arms out to King.

Carlton stood and walked to the bar. He grabbed a glass and poured her a drink.

"Hey baby, I thought I heard someone come in. It's good to see you," Yogi said, hugging her son tightly.

King felt the anger and despair that had consumed him moments ago lift as his mother hugged him.

Carlton touched her back and handed her the glass.

Yogi flashed a smile at him and kissed his cheek. "Well, I will let you men get back to business," Yogi said, making her way towards the stairs. "Oh, and Sunday dinner will be served at four. I don't care how late you are out tonight, you better not be late."

King laughed and nodded.

His mother cut her eyes at him playfully and blew him a kiss.

"Night, Ma," King said as she walked back up the stairs.